"I'm hav
a wond

Hannah linked her fingers behind Trace's neck as they swayed to the music. "I'm also flattered to be in the company of Arizona's Lawman of the Year."

He didn't want to talk about his work. Not when his body was responding to her closeness. "It's no big deal."

Tilting her head, she looked up at him. "Being a hero's no big deal?" Once again she rested her head against his shoulder, sighing happily as their bodies melded. "Do you have any idea how few women get a date with a full-fledged hero? I feel like Lois Lane."

"Just don't get your hopes up too high," he warned, pushing aside her hair, allowing his lips access to her neck. "I can't leap tall buildings in a single bound."

"I certainly wouldn't expect you to."

"And I'm definitely not faster than a speeding bullet."

"Believe me, Trace," she murmured seductively, "you've no idea how happy I am to hear you say that."

JoAnn Ross says she had three reasons for writing *Murphy's Law*, her fifteenth Temptation. "First, I wanted to celebrate small-town values. Second, many books in the romance genre feature two people who are divorced because of unhappy marriages. I wanted to write a book with two people who were both happily married and now are dealing with a new relationship. And third, I love to cook, and one of my fantasies, like that of Hannah, the heroine, is to own a restaurant."

JoAnn lives with her husband in Phoenix, Arizona.

Books by JoAnn Ross

HARLEQUIN TEMPTATION

153–TEMPTING FATE
171–HOT ON THE TRAIL
187–WORTH WAITING FOR
193–SPIRIT OF LOVE
201–IN A CLASS BY HIMSELF
209–WILDE 'N' WONDERFUL
221–EVE'S CHOICE

Murphy's Law
JoANN ROSS

Harlequin Books

TORONTO • NEW YORK • LONDON
AMSTERDAM • PARIS • SYDNEY • HAMBURG
STOCKHOLM • ATHENS • TOKYO • MILAN

Published January 1989

ISBN 0-373-25333-8

1

"THE BID is fifteen hundred and sixty dollars. Do we have fifteen-seventy? Seventy-five? Who'll give me fifteen-eighty?"

Hannah Greene stood silently at the back of the wainscoted room, her gray eyes resolutely dry as she watched the past fourteen years of her life being sold off piece by piece. The thick cloud of Giorgio hovering overhead was beginning to make her head ache.

When she was a little girl growing up in Iowa, her parents had encouraged her to believe in fairy tales. An obedient child, Hannah willingly complied. At nineteen, armed with a diploma from the Cedar Rapids Business School, she bought a ticket on a Greyhound bus and went to New York, where she got a job working as a Girl Friday for a prince of a man named David Greene.

On their first date, she and David decided they wanted to have children together; on their second, David proposed, and Hannah moved into his three-room castle in Flatbush. As the years went by, David's business grew by leaps and bounds, allowing them to move into a larger palace in Connecticut where Scott—heir to the Greene Advertising throne—was born.

The only problem with fairy tales, Hannah had discovered, was that they didn't warn you that the prince could die of a perforated ulcer, the creditors could end up with the castle, and it could be back to the ashes for Cinderella.

"Ladies and gentlemen," the dapper auctioneer cajoled winningly, "may I remind you that this table is in excellent condition. Even without the matching chairs, it could be considered a steal at two thousand."

Remembering the years of celebratory dinners shared around the elegant dining-room set, Hannah wondered how anyone could put a price on love. She'd worked the Regency-style floral needlepoint covers for the chairs herself that long-ago winter when she had been pregnant with Scott. David, flushed with the glow of impending fatherhood and concerned for her health, had insisted she quit working. Bored, she'd taught herself needlework to pass the long hours spent waiting for her husband's return from his Madison Avenue advertising agency.

"Fifteen-seventy-five," the auctioneer conceded when his efforts were met by a stony wall of silence. "Going once, twice, gone to the lady in the red hat. The next item going up for bid is a superb-quality George III satinwood bookcase."

"You look as if you could use a break," Janet Morrison murmured as the workmen carried the dining-room set from the dais.

"I'm fine," Hannah insisted, her gaze directed toward the bookcase. She and David had discovered it in a little out-of-the-way shop in London the summer Scott turned two. They'd justified the hefty purchase price by telling each other that the bookcase would become a family heirloom; something their son would pass on to his own children.

"Well, I for one am in desperate need of a cigarette," Janet said. "Come keep me company." Taking Hannah by the arm, she practically dragged her out of the library, down the long terrazzo hallway and out onto the back terrace.

"I thought the doctor warned you to give those things up if you wanted a speedy recovery," Hannah reminded her long-time friend and neighbor.

Janet lit a slender cigarette with a gold lighter and exhaled a long breath of relief. "I still have a few weeks until my surgery. Besides, everyone I know gains at least ten pounds when they quit smoking. I'm attempting to forestall the inevitable as long as possible."

At forty-eight, Janet Morrison was fifteen years older than Hannah. Her honeyed complexion was nearly flawless, save for the small network of lines fanning outward from her eyes and the slight bracketing around her russet-tinted lips. Like so many other women in the neighborhood, Janet was resolutely fit, tanned and blond. Cursed with fair skin that refused to tan and poker-straight black hair, Hannah had, on more than one occasion, envied her best friend.

"I still can't figure out why you feel you need a face-lift," she said honestly. "I think you look great."

"Sure, that's easy for you to say," Janet retorted. "Your husband didn't just hire a new secretary who looks as if she should be leading cheers for the high-school football team." The words were no sooner out of her mouth than Janet groaned. "Oh, Hannah, I'm sorry. It just slipped out."

Hannah could feel her lips smiling, but inside she remained numb, as she had for the past eighteen months. "Don't worry about it. I'm fine. Really."

It was Janet Morrison's turn to submit Hannah to a lengthy examination. "No," she said finally, "you're not. Oh, you've been putting on a good show, but anyone who truly knows you could see that you've just been going through the motions. Although it's no wonder, considering the mess David left behind."

Hannah didn't answer immediately. Instead, she looked out over the acres of serene, unspoiled woodland, realizing that this would be the last time she'd be able to enjoy the view. The trees were wearing their autumnal coats of red and gold and bronze, and from her hilltop vantage point, she could see the free-flowing stream cutting through the brilliantly colored forest. Come winter the stream would freeze solid, but for the moment it tumbled merrily over moss-covered rocks, oblivious of its fate.

"Do you remember when I began volunteering one day a week down at the food-stamp office?" she asked suddenly.

"Of course, I didn't really believe that there *were* any food-stamp recipients in Connecticut."

"I know. You asked me to bring a few extra stamps home for pâté and caviar."

"We were having a party that weekend and every little bit helps. Is this little trip down memory lane leading anywhere?"

Hannah dragged her hand through her hair. Her simple gold wedding band—the only piece of jewelry she hadn't sold—gleamed in the midafternoon sun. "I met so many women there—women who'd led lives of convenience and comfort—who were suddenly forced into dire financial straits due to their husband's death. Or a divorce.

"These were not underprivileged individuals, and they were intelligent, well educated. Yet each had made the mistake of allowing her husband to make all the decisions, to handle the money without her knowledge or consent. I felt sorry for them, but inside, I couldn't help feeling a little smug, you know? Because David and I always shared everything." Her soft laugh was without humor. "At least I thought we shared everything."

"Honey, you had no way of knowing David's business was in such a slump. It's obvious he was only trying to protect you."

That was the same thing Hannah had been trying to tell herself over and over again these past months as she'd struggled to pay off the debts that her husband had incurred. Unfortunately, she hadn't reaped any financial rewards by understanding David's motivation.

"I know. I just wish he'd trusted me enough to come to me with his problems."

Janet put her hand on Hannah's arm. "And what could you have done?"

Looking down at her friend's perfectly manicured hand, it occurred to Hannah that her own nails were, as usual these days, ragged and unpolished. "The same thing I'm doing now," she answered without hesitation. "Selling the Manhattan apartment, the house, the furniture, the jewelry, taking Scotty out of private school, going back to work."

"That's not the life David wanted for you."

This time Hannah's smile was unmistakably grim. "Well, like it or not, it's the life I ended up with. The only difference is, if he'd bothered to ask me, I would have told him that I'd rather go back to our first apartment than continue living in Connecticut without him."

"He undoubtedly figured he could turn the business around."

Hannah exhaled a soft, rippling little sigh. "I know. And he would have, if it hadn't killed him first."

Both women remained silent for a time, staring out over the rolling expanse of lawn. The tennis court needed work, Hannah mused. The red clay was badly scuffed and covered with debris. Dead leaves floated on the swimming pool because she kept forgetting to cover it.

"So," Janet said finally, stubbing out her cigarette, "how's Scotty taking the move?"

"I thought he'd be upset about changing schools again and leaving all his friends behind, but all he talks about is moving to the wild west. In fact, not only have cowboys replaced the Yankees in his eight-year-old hierarchy, I haven't had to listen to a Spiderman or Masters of the Universe plot for six weeks."

"Kids are resilient."

"Isn't that the truth? You'd never know that his world had been turned upside down." Hannah was grateful for her son's apparent ability to bounce back from what had been a disastrous eighteen months.

"How about you?" Janet asked softly. "How are you holding up?"

Hannah took her time in answering. A covey of quail was bobbing across the lawn, and she found herself envying them their close-knit little group. Drawing in a breath, she leaned her head against one of five white wooden posts supporting the slate roof. The post bore the inscription David Loves Hannah. Encouraged by a bit too much champagne, her husband had carved the romantic declaration the weekend they'd moved into the house nine years ago.

"I'm fine. Really."

Her friend gave her a long, judicious look. "You're still too thin, but I think you are beginning to look a little less tense. And either you've discovered some miracle cosmetic I don't know about, or the circles under your eyes are finally gone."

"I've been sleeping better lately." Ever since she'd made the decision to move to Arizona, Hannah thought. "Sometimes all through the night."

"Well, that's something. Did you finally break down and take my advice?"

"Advice?"

"About seeing Larry Newman."

Dr. Lawrence Newman was president of the country club and on the board of directors of several hospitals, as well as being the leading local psychiatrist. There were probably very few people in Hannah's circle he hadn't seen on a professional basis, causing David Greene to have once suggested that if the good doctor ever decided to write his memoirs, the book would probably sell out in Greenwich within ten minutes.

"I had one appointment."

"Really? How did it go?"

Hannah shrugged. "It didn't. I didn't go back."

"If it's the money, I can lend you Larry's fee."

Janet knew it would be useless to offer to give Hannah the funds outright. If there was anything the past eighteen months had proven, it was that Hannah Greene's pride was a formidable thing. Ignoring legal advice to declare bankruptcy, and thus get out from under the burden of her husband's business responsibilities, Hannah had insisted on paying off every last dollar, at considerable personal sacrifice.

"It's not the money." Hannah's cheeks burned as she remembered the look of pity on the psychiatrist's handsome face. After the pity had come the inevitable pass.

"Larry hit on you, didn't he?" Janet said knowingly.

"You don't sound surprised."

"Hannah, practically every woman at the club has had an affair with the guy."

"You're kidding."

"Not at all. Don't tell me you didn't notice? Ever since he moved to Greenwich, there's been enough hanky-panky going on to provide three season's worth of Dynasty scripts."

"I never knew," Hannah murmured, wondering if Janet had actually participated in any of the alleged hanky-panky.

"How could you, since whenever you and David showed up at any functions, the two of you couldn't keep your eyes—or your hands—off each other." Janet shook her head as she lit another cigarette. "Honestly, sweetie, the way you two carried on threatened to give marriage a bad name. Didn't anyone ever tell you wide-eyed innocents that lust is supposed to die by the first anniversary?"

"And love? When does that die?"

"By the fifth. At least."

"I never stopped loving David."

"Nor he you. That's what made the two of you a throwback to some other time. It's also what made the rest of us jealous as hell." Janet observed Hannah through a cloud of blue smoke. She'd brought her out here for a much-needed respite from the pain of watching her personal belongings being auctioned off to strangers. Unfortunately, the conversation was getting decidedly depressing. "So, when do you leave for Last Chance?"

"It's New Chance," Hannah corrected faintly. "And we're leaving first thing in the morning."

"So soon? I thought you were staying until Friday."

"In case you didn't notice, our beds were sold out from under us in the first hour this morning. Hotels cost money."

"So stay with us."

"Thanks, but I really want to spend this last night alone with Scotty. In case he suddenly gets depressed about leaving the only home he's ever known and wants to talk about it."

"Look, I understand why you want to open your own restaurant," Janet said. "You've gone to cooking school, you've catered every party around here for the past five years, even before you started charging, and everyone loves your food. But what in the hell made you decide on Arizona? What's wrong with Manhattan? Or Connecticut?"

"In the first place, I could never afford to open a restaurant in Manhattan. And Connecticut isn't that much better. For what it would cost me to pay six month's rent in the city, I was able to buy the Red Rock Café outright. And have enough left over for a year's rent on a house."

"Both sight unseen," Janet reminded her.

"The real estate agent sent photographs of the café," Hannah said, remembering the blurred, indistinct Polaroids the saleswoman had forwarded after Hannah had responded to the listing in the Wall Street Journal. "I'll admit it looks as if it could use a little work, but it's rather . . . quaint."

"Quaint," Janet sniffed. "That sounds like real estate jargon for a dump. Along the lines of a Honeymoon Special. Or Handyman Fix-up. For heaven's sake, Hannah, just because David died doesn't mean you have to banish yourself to the wilderness."

"I'm not banishing myself," Hannah said, repeating the words she'd been saying to herself since she'd come up with the idea six months ago. "I'm starting a new life." Although she'd never admit it, the name of the small Arizona community—New Chance—had been what had first attracted her to the advertisement.

"So, start a new life here," Janet insisted. "Open your restaurant, begin dating again, try having some fun for a change."

"I tried dating, remember?" Her one-time excursion into the singles world, with the agent who'd listed her Manhattan apartment, had turned out to be an unqualified disaster.

Janet shrugged. "So, Bernie was a bust. There are lots more fish in the sea, Hannah."

"I'm not into angling these days, Jan. I only want to make a new life in Arizona for myself and my son."

Janet Morrison stubbed out her cigarette. "I'm really going to miss you," she said, throwing her arms around Hannah.

Moisture stung her eyelids as Hannah returned the hug. "And I'm going to miss you."

"We'll come visit," Janet insisted as they parted.

"By next summer I should have the restaurant running well enough to take a few days off," Hannah said. "We'll drive up to the Grand Canyon."

"Next summer," Janet confirmed.

"Definitely," Hannah agreed. "It's a date."

Both women's smiles were brittle. False. And as they walked back into the house, both knew that in spite of their good intentions, their lives, which had been entwined for so many years, were inexorably drifting apart.

THE RED ROCK CAFÉ was a wreck. Which wasn't all that surprising, Trace Murphy considered as he stepped over the heavy fire hoses and sloshed through three inches of blackened water. Fires had a way of making things downright messy. Although the flames had been extinguished, a thick cloud of acrid smoke hung heavily over the restaurant, stinging his eyes and scorching his throat.

He found the three remaining members of the volunteer fire department in the kitchen, drinking coffee. Amazingly, the enormous stainless-steel urn had escaped the fire unharmed.

"Hey, Trace," Cal Potter greeted him with a grin that appeared broad and white in his blackened face, "you're just in time for cleanup."

Trace waded through the grimy water to the pot and wished he was wearing his weekend work boots. Wet soot had already darkened the silver lizardskin to a muddy gray. "My timing's always been terrific," he said as he poured coffee into a chipped white mug.

"Speaking of timing, what do you think Mitzi's gonna do when she finds out about this?" Fred Wiley asked. The volunteer fireman's face was as dark and streaked as his partner's.

"Mitzi?" Trace tasted the coffee and understood why the coffeepot had escaped destruction. If it could hold the battery acid that Johnny Mott called coffee, it had to be lined with one of those new miracle petroleum products.

"Do you think she's going to notify that woman?" Fred asked.

"What woman?"

"You know, the Easterner who bought this place?"

"Her name's Hannah Greene," said Dan Murphy, former Mingus County sheriff and Trace's father.

"Oh, her." Trace shrugged. "I suppose it'd only be the right thing to do, considering." His green eyes swept the room, taking in the destruction.

Water was everywhere—on the floor, the counters, the six-burner stove, the oversize dual sinks. The oak countertop was already beginning to swell from the abundance of moisture. By tomorrow, it would be warped beyond repair. The overhead hood, designed to handle a reasonable amount of smoke, had been completely blackened and the industrial green paint on the walls had blistered badly.

"Where's Johnny?"

"Al drove him to the hospital in Cottonwood. We were worried that all this smoke might bring on an attack of his emphysema," Dan said.

"Is he in bad shape?"

His father shrugged. "Didn't seem much worse than usual. I suspect what's really bothering him is worry that the sale will fall through."

"Mitzi should call that buyer," Cal Potter said, unable to resist putting in his two cents' worth. "Especially with her being a widow lady and all. Finding this mess waiting for her would be bad enough even if she did have a man to help her get the place put back together again."

"Yep, Mitzi's gonna have to call her," Wiley agreed with a broad nod of his grizzled gray head. "Even if it does mean giving up her commission."

"She can't," Dan Murphy said.

"She already spent the money?" Potter asked with a look that suggested *ain't that just like a woman?*

"It's got nothing to do with the money," Dan said. "The reason Mitzi can't call the Greene woman is because she's already left Connecticut. In fact, she's scheduled to arrive here today."

For the past six months, Dan Murphy had, in the local vernacular, been keeping company with Mitzi Patterson, New Chance's sole real estate agent. Since Mitzi also served as social reporter for the *New Chance Clarion*, Dan was in a position to know more than he wanted to about the town's goings-on.

Cal Potter and Fred Wiley whistled in unison at the news. "Wouldn't want to be the one who's got to tell the little lady that she's bought herself a pig in a poke," Wiley muttered.

"Me neither," Potter agreed.

Dan Murphy remained silent and looked grim.

Trace Murphy was looking out the front window. A car had pulled up in front of the café, a green Volvo station wagon with Connecticut plates. "Looks like somebody's gonna have to break the news," he said.

Three pairs of eyes followed his to the street. Silence settled over the ravaged kitchen.

"I think Trace should be the one," Potter said finally.

"Me, too," Wiley added, seconding the motion.

Trace hooked his thumbs in the pocket of his jeans and frowned. He had served for eight years in the Marines; six of those years as a sergeant in the military police. During his time in the armed forces, he'd served in Lebanon and Central America. After returning to civilian life, he put in three years in the Phoenix police department, working night patrols in high-crime districts. In all those years of working in high-risk situations, he'd never—not once—considered himself a coward. Until now.

"Why me?" he asked.

"Seem's reasonable to me," Dan Murphy drawled. "Seein' as how you're the sheriff, and all."

Keeping law and order in Mingus County was one thing. Telling a widow who had driven all the way across the country that her dream had just gone up in smoke was quite another. Trace took another fortifying drink of coffee and wished it was something stronger. That is, if anything short of toxic waste was stronger than Johnny Mott's coffee.

"I don't suppose I have any choice."

"Don't suppose you do," Dan Murphy murmured.

Although Dan's tone remained noncommittal, a fleeting look of sympathy appeared in his eyes, making Trace remember the winter when he was seven and his father had been called away from dinner to tell Mrs. Vance that her husband wouldn't be coming home for Christmas. Ed Vance's logging truck had hit a patch of black ice and skidded out of control on the switchbacks between Flagstaff and Sedona. Then there'd been the time that Billy Duncan had drowned in Potter's Pond and Dan had held a hysterical Karen Duncan in his arms, rocking her like a child, murmuring inarticulate words of comfort until she'd run out of tears. There had been other such instances during Dan Murphy's twenty-five-year tenure as sheriff. More than Trace could count.

"Guess it comes with the territory," he said unenthusiastically.

"Guess it does," Dan agreed.

This time it was pride Trace viewed in his father's eyes. Pride and empathy. He drew in a deep breath and put the chipped mug down on the muddy counter. "Well, here goes nothing."

HANNAH CLENCHED the steering wheel as she stared out the window at the Red Rock Café. Although from outside there was no sign of the destruction awaiting her within, the scene that greeted her was not encouraging.

"Well, it's certainly appropriately named," she said with feigned cheer as she took in the small square building constructed out of varying sizes and shapes of red rocks held together with dark gray mortar.

"The cow's neat," her eight-year-old son offered.

Despite her best intentions, Hannah couldn't help cringing as she raised her eyes to the life-size statue of a brown cow atop the roof. A cow that Mitzi Patterson's

Polaroid photograph had failed to reveal. "Well, it's different, at any rate."

"Wait till Jimmy finds out we own a restaurant with a cow on the roof," Scott said enthusiastically. "He'll never believe it. Can I call him long-distance tonight, Mom? And tell him about the cow?"

"I suppose so," Hannah murmured, staring up at the cow. It was so horribly large. "Let's check out the inside," she suggested. "We'll have a nice brunch and take a tour of the kitchen before going to Ms Patterson's office to pick up the key to our house."

"Do you think the house will have a cow on the roof, too?"

"I fervently hope not."

"Maybe it'll have a horse," Scott suggested. "Wouldn't that be neat?"

"Neat," Hannah agreed absently.

She'd just gotten out of the car and was headed toward the café, Scott at her heels, when Trace Murphy walked out the door. Stunned, Hannah came to an abrupt halt.

The man was, in a word, perfect. Impossibly, magnificently perfect. His face was tanned to the color of hazelnuts, his jaw was firm, chin ruggedly square and marked by a deep and delicious cleft. His nose was straight, and his eyes, beneath the brim of a fawn-colored Stetson, were a remarkable green so bright that were the rest of him not flawless, she might have suspected him of wearing tinted contacts. It was as if the Marlboro man had suddenly sprung to life and walked off a billboard.

While Hannah was absorbing every stunning aspect of Trace's physical appearance, he was, in turn, trying not to stare as he approached her. This was the widow lady? An educated guess put her age somewhere in her early thirties, which was about three decades younger than he'd

imagined. Her hair, tied back at her nape was neither white
nor gray, but a smooth and gleaming ebony. Her skin was
ivory, reminding him of the porcelain dolls his great-great-
grandmother had insisted on bringing across the country
in their covered wagon, against all odds of their surviv-
ing the journey intact.

"Mrs. Greene?" he asked hesitantly. Trace still could not
quite believe that this woman in the stone-washed jeans
and oversize sweatshirt was the one they'd been talking
about only minutes earlier.

His voice was a lush, deep baritone that was as improb-
ably faultless as his rugged good looks. For a brief, fleeting moment Hannah imagined showing up with this man
at the country club. The women would all go wild; it'd be
like throwing him into a bucket with a school of starving
piranha. That image made her smile.

"I'm Hannah Greene," she said, holding out her hand.

It was the smile that did it, making her appear even
younger, warming her dark eyes, and causing a glow to
spread over her skin. As Trace took her hand he stared,
momentarily transfixed.

"Are you a cowboy?" Scott asked, staring up at the tall
man in the Stetson.

"Not really." Trace watched the disappointment move
across the freckled young face. "But I am sheriff of Mingus County."

Scott beamed. "A real live sheriff," he said, "Holy cow.
Wait'll Jimmy Walker hears about this."

"Jimmy is Scotty's best friend," Hannah explained.
"Back home in Connecticut." Not that Connecticut was
home any longer, she reminded herself. This was home
now. This restaurant with the enormous brown cow on the
roof.

"I figured as much." He'd yet to release her hand, but since the lady hadn't seen fit to object, Trace decided that there was no point in rushing things. Using his free hand, he took off his hat, revealing thick chestnut hair gilded with streaks of gold by the sun. Hannah instantly decided that it was unfair for a man to be gifted with such physical beauty. "I'm Trace Murphy."

"It's a pleasure to meet you, Sheriff. This is my son, Scotty."

"Mom," Scott said on a loud stage whisper, "I keep telling you, you have to call me Scott. I'm the man of the house, now," he explained to Trace. "And Scotty's just a little kid's name."

Relinquishing possession of the mother, Trace held his hand out to the son. "Hi, Scott. Welcome to New Chance."

"My mom and me came to Arizona to start a new life," Scott revealed.

"My mom and I," Hannah corrected, her eyes glued to the roof.

Up close, the cow appeared even more gargantuan. She blinked slowly, hoping that when she looked again the enormous brown animal would prove to be merely a figment of her imagination, brought on by exhaustion and too many hours staring at the seemingly endless miles of asphalt crossing the country. No such luck. When she opened her eyes again, the cow was still there in all its bovine glory.

Scott shrugged off the murmured grammar lesson. "Anyway, my mom and *I* bought this restaurant because she's the best cook in the whole world. Everyone thinks so. Not just me. Wait till you taste her pot roast. It's scrumptious."

"I'm looking forward to it."

"Dad always said it was great—even better than Gram's."

"If your dad said so, I'm sure it's true."

"It is. Gram died. So did my Grandma and Grandpa Field—they were my mom's mom and dad—but that was a long time ago, when I was just a baby, so I don't remember them, except from the old home movies Mom keeps in the bookcase. My dad died, too, so we're all alone now, but we have each other. Right, Mom?"

"Right." Dragging her eyes from the roof, Hannah decided to call a halt to this increasingly uncomfortable conversation before Scott proceeded to reveal her entire life story. "Well, as nice as it's been talking with you, Sheriff Murphy," she said, "I'd like to inspect my café."

Trace hoped that Hannah Greene was tougher than she looked, because the widow lady was going to need every bit of strength she possessed. And then some.

"Sure. Come on in and I'll show you around."

"I appreciate your offer, Sheriff, but you needn't bother. Surely giving restaurant tours isn't part of your job."

"The name's Trace," he corrected, taking her elbow as he shepherded her toward the front door. "And as for this being part of the job, Hannah, I'm afraid that it is."

2

"OH, NO!" Hannah's eyes widened in dismay as she stared at the wreckage that greeted her entry into the restaurant.

The brown tile floor was awash with soot and ashes, and acrid smoke hung over the room like a funeral pall. Which was appropriate, Hannah decided. Because the devastation represented the death of a dream that had been keeping her going for months.

"Gee," Scott murmured, his eyes wide, dark saucers. "It looks even worse than the time Peter Martin's science project exploded inside the microwave."

"I'm afraid the kitchen is in even worse shape," Trace said quietly, watching Hannah carefully for signs that she might be about to faint.

"I find that hard to believe," she murmured, her gaze sweeping the room, taking in the smoke-tinged walls, the blackened ceiling, the sodden green felt of the pool table in the corner. Her already fair skin paled to the color of newly driven snow.

"Perhaps you should go back outside in the fresh air and sit down for a while," Trace suggested solicitously.

It was his tone that did it—sympathy, tinged with just enough pity to trigger a lingering vestige of pride. Hannah had heard that tone directed her way more times than she'd care to count over the past year and a half. Reminding herself that the reason she had come to Arizona, the reason she had dragged an eight-year-old child nearly all the way across the country, was to escape just such solicitude, she went rigid: arms, back, resolve.

"I believe I'd like to see the kitchen," she said, meeting his concerned look with a calm, level one of her own.

Trace tipped the brim of his hat back with his thumb, eyeing her with a mixture of admiration and concern. "Now it's not that I want to stand in your way, but I'm not sure that'd be a real good idea, Hannah," he said, his deep voice coaxing the feminine acquiescence he was accustomed to receiving from the most strong-willed of females. "Believe me, it's an unholy mess back there."

After what she'd been through, Hannah refused to allow a bit—all right, she admitted, more than a bit—of smoke and water to get the best of her.

"I believe you, Sheriff," she said. "But you see, unholy or not, it *is* my mess." With that she brushed passed him, pushing aside the swinging doors that led to the kitchen.

Well, she thought, taking in the destruction that made the outer room look neat and tidy by comparison, Trace Murphy definitely couldn't be accused of exaggerating about the kitchen.

And at the very center of the muck and mire was a group of three men who were all staring at her with varying amounts of interest. Fred Wiley bit through the cigar he'd just lighted.

"Good morning, gentlemen," she greeted them, forcing a smile that only wobbled slightly.

"Good morning, ma'am," Cal Potter said. He yanked off his hat and gave her a stilted bow such as he might have bestowed on Princess Di, were the Princess of Wales to have paid a royal visit to New Chance.

"Morning," Wiley mumbled, staring down at his boots as he plucked bits of tobacco out of his mouth.

"Mrs. Greene," Dan said, extending a hand, "I'm Dan Murphy, and those gentlemen are Cal Potter and Fred Wiley, two members of New Chance's Volunteer Fire Department. Cal's also Mingus County's deputy sheriff and Fred runs Wiley's Feed and Grain.

"It's a real pleasure to meet you, ma'am, although I wish it could have been under more pleasant circumstances."

"I certainly can't argue with you there," Hannah murmured, as her hand disappeared into Dan Murphy's. When she felt the calluses brush against her palm, she thought how much the handshake reminded her of the one she'd experienced outside, with New Chance's sheriff. "Murphy," she said thoughtfully, "are you . . ."

"My father," Trace filled in for her. "And former sheriff of New Chance."

Eyeing Dan Murphy with renewed interest, Hannah realized that had she not been so stunned by the devastation of the Red Rock Café's kitchen, she would have spotted the resemblance immediately. Dan Murphy's tanned face was older, and more weathered by the elements, and his hair was frosted with silver rather than gold, but there was no mistaking the square jaw, the firm lips and those incredible green eyes that recalled sunlight shining on a newly mown meadow. He was a remarkably handsome man for someone she guessed was in his early sixties.

"I can see the resemblance," she said.

Dan's answering grin lit up the room, making Hannah wonder if his son also possessed such a dazzling power. "Lots of folks say that," he said. "That's when I always point out that I'm the good-looking one."

"And modest, too," Trace murmured.

"Hell, son, no point hiding your light under a bushel. Not when there's a pretty woman around, anyway." His laughing gaze paid her a masculine compliment before moving beyond Hannah to the wide-eyed boy standing in the doorway. "You must be Scott. We're pleased as punch to have you in New Chance. The town's in need of young blood."

"How did you know my name?"

"Mitzi told me. She's been going on and on about you and your mom. There's nothing that woman loves more than helping young families settle in."

"Are you a cowboy?" Scott asked, eyeing the black hat atop Dan Murhpy's head.

"Well," Dan said consideringly, "if owning a few head of mangy, mean old cattle makes a man a cowboy, I suppose I am."

"Wow," Scott breathed appreciatively, looking up at his mother. "A sheriff and a cowboy. All in the first day. What a great place. Huh, Mom?"

"Great," Hannah answered absently. She'd only been vaguely aware of the conversation as she studied the kitchen with the eye of a woman who might be down, but wasn't about to be counted out, yet.

"How did the fire start?" she asked. "Was it the wiring?"

"Nothing that serious, ma'am," Cal Potter assured her, assuming his role as chief of the volunteer fire department. "You see, Johnny—he's the one who owns the place—is getting on in years."

"So Ms Patterson told me," Hannah said. "I believe she also said that he was selling the restaurant so he could move to California to live with his son and daughter-in-law."

"And their five kids," Dan added. "Johnny's had a real hankering to be a live-in grandpa ever since John junior came to town for the Fourth of July celebrations and invited his daddy back to Bakersfield."

He shook his head as he looked around the room. They'd opened the back door and most of the smoke had drifted out onto the autumn breeze, but instead of making the place look better, the bright November sunlight only highlighted the devastation.

"It'd be a crying shame if he doesn't get to make the trip. What with his emphysema and all, no telling how long the poor old guy's got."

Trace shot his father a suspicious look. It was not at all Dan Murphy's style to play games of emotional blackmail, but damned if that wasn't what he seemed to be doing.

"I can imagine," Hannah murmured. "And I sympathize with Mr. Mott and his son and each and every one of his five grandchildren. But you still haven't told me how the fire started."

"Grease trap," Wiley said, as though he'd decided he'd been left out of the conversation long enough. "Damn fool forgot to clean it out last week."

"That's all it was? An overfilled grease trap?"

"That's about it," Cal agreed, shooting Fred Wiley a sharp look obviously intended to remind him exactly who was the official spokesman for the group.

"So, what you're saying is that if Mr. Mott had remembered to clean out the grease trap, this fire never would have occurred."

Cal Potter gave her a look that suggested she'd just answered the sixty-four-thousand-dollar question. "That's it, exactly. The wiring's fine, ma'am. My brother Hal, well, he's an electrician over in Cottonwood and he installed that new stove and hood for Johnny just last winter. He also checked out the rest of the wiring and said it was shipshape."

"I suppose your brother would know."

"Oh, yes, ma'am. He knows the electrical business inside out. The county inspector gave the job a green tag first time out."

Hannah nodded thoughtfully as she reached up and ran her finger along the blackened overhead hood. She decided that several buckets of Mr. Clean and hot water should return it to its gleaming copper glory. The countertops looked as though they were beyond repair, but she would have wanted to replace the scarred oak, anyway. The paint was blistered; the walls would have to be scraped and sanded, but from what she could tell, the color had been a muddy military green that would have made her feel as if she were cooking in a MASH unit.

"I take it the restaurant is insured," she said.

Cal Potter nervously cleared his throat.

Fred Wiley returned to his previous mute state and took a sudden interest in digging soot from beneath his grime-encrusted fingernails with a pocketknife.

Dan Murphy took off his hat and began finger-combing his wavy silver hair.

The silence was deafening.

"I'm afraid it's not," Dan said finally. "You see, the policy was up for renewal last week and Johnny just—"

"Forgot to pay the renewal premium," Hannah interrupted.

"That's about it in a nutshell," Dan admitted. "But you know, if you'd still be willing to buy the Red Rock, I'm sure Mitzi could work out some sort of compromise price."

Even as Hannah considered the magnitude of such a challenge, she was forced to ask herself what choice she had. She couldn't go back to Connecticut; her house and all her possessions were gone. She had no family, no ties anywhere else. The truth was, she'd pinned all her hopes on New Chance. Like it or not, New Chance was her *only* chance.

"I don't know," she murmured, opening a cupboard and finding it filled with heavy white plates, all of them chipped. "Without insurance . . ."

Trace felt her wavering and wondered why he was rooting for her to stay when it was obvious that she was facing overwhelming odds if she did decide to try to make a go of it.

"New Chance is a real friendly town, Mrs. Greene," Dan said encouragingly. "We do things here a little different than you're probably used to in the city. I guarantee you that if you decide to stay, we'll all chip in."

"My brother would be glad to donate his services," Cal Potter assured her with a big grin. The noonday sun, pouring in through the open door, glinted on his gold front tooth. "And I'm right handy with a hammer and nails."

"I've been promising the wife I'd paint the parlor all summer," Fred Wiley mumbled. "I don't suppose it'd make no difference if it waited a few more months. If you'd like some white paint."

"I'm an old hand at refinishing wood," Dan said. "With a little linseed oil and some elbow grease, we could get those cabinets back to tip-top condition in no time."

"Hank Young, down at Young's Hardware, still owes me from last Saturday night's poker game," Trace heard himself saying. "Hank's a real nice guy, but he's got an unfortunate tendency to draw on an inside straight—he'd probably be more than happy to donate some roofing material."

Hannah could hardly believe her ears. After David's death, she'd received innumerable offers of assistance. But all of them had been prefaced with the words, "If there's anything I can do." There had been a great deal those well-meaning individuals could have done to ease the burden Hannah had found herself facing, but when it came to actually requesting specific favors, she had choked on her damnable pride.

This time, however, four men, all virtual strangers, were offering specific solutions to her problems. It was as wonderful as it was incredible.

"Why?" she asked softly. "Why would you all be willing to help a stranger?"

"If you decide to stay in New Chance, Mrs. Greene," Dan said simply, "you won't be a stranger."

"That's right," Cal agreed. "You'll be one of us."

"And New Chance takes care of its own," Wiley put in.

Trace remained silent, watching her carefully, waiting for her answer. Out of the corner of his eye, he could see her son shifting anxiously from foot to foot as he, too, watched her.

"I believe I would like to talk to Ms Patterson," Hannah decided at length.

"She had to go into Phoenix," Dan said. "She just sold her own house down there—took her six months to decide to list it, then damned if it didn't sell the very first weekend. Of course she was a mite upset when the title company wanted to close on the house today, with you coming to town and all. But I promised I'd take care of things."

"I can certainly understand why she had to leave town, but about our rental house . . ."

"Don't worry, she gave me the key this morning." Potter and Wiley's muffled snorts of laughter drew a warning glare from Dan. "It's not what you old coots are thinking.

Mitzi and I had breakfast right here at the Red Rock before she left."

The two men's eyes turned guileless, but the laughter didn't fade. "Did we say anything to the contrary, Dan?" Potter asked.

"Just see that you don't," Dan grumbled, knowing full well that his love life had been the favorite topic down at Harry Banks's barber shop lately. "Anyway," he said, turning back to Hannah, "Mitzi asked me to help you and your youngster get all settled in. Then you and she can discuss your real-estate deal over dinner out at my place."

"I wouldn't want to put you out," Hannah demurred. Although she appreciated the gesture, she was slightly uncomfortable with the gregariousness of the townspeople she'd met so far.

Dan laughed. A deep, robust sound that she was certain the absent Mitzi found more than a little attractive. "Hell, Hannah, the day I turn down a chance to spend time with a pretty woman is the day they can start measuring me for a funeral suit. Right, son?"

Trace returned the smile, but his gaze was directed straight at Hannah. "Right," he answered absently.

As his green eyes took a slow, leisurely tour of her face, Hannah remained as still as a statue, deciding to humor the man, even as she sought to pretend such blatantly masculine appraisal was a common, everyday occurrence.

She was just priding herself on her success when those brilliant green eyes settled on her lips and lingered, as if imagining their warmth, their taste. The quick, spontaneous pull his look incited was every bit as unexpected as it was undeniable. Her mouth suddenly went dry; she resisted the almost overwhelming urge to lick her lips.

"Well," she said brightly as she glanced vaguely around the kitchen, "I suppose I've seen enough for now."

Dan, who had not missed the look that had passed between Hannah and his son, decided that if the widow Greene could be convinced to stay, there would soon be a hot new topic of conversation down at Harry's.

"We'll get you all settled in in no time," he said, rubbing his broad, dark hands together with pleasure. "Trace, why don't you come along," he suggested casually. "An extra hand's always good to have around on moving day."

Trace was well aware that his father was manipulating the situation, throwing him and Hannah together in a heavy-handed attempt at matchmaking. Still, he decided with an inward shrug, he was the sheriff. He'd only be doing his duty helping a young widow and her son get settled.

"I'd be glad to help," he said.

"That's very nice of you, Sheriff," Hannah said quickly. "But I'm sure you must have far more important things to do than carry boxes."

"None that I can think of at the moment, ma'am," Trace assured her, matching her polite tone. "If you decide to stay, you'll discover things are pretty peaceful around New Chance."

"Well, let's get going," Dan said heartily, putting a friendly arm around Scott's shoulders.

As Hannah returned to the Volvo parked at the curb, she considered that despite the fire, despite the fact that the Red Rock Café was far from the quaint western eatery Mitzi Patterson had made it out to be, despite the fact that Trace Murphy made her feel something she had no business feeling, despite all that, she just might have found her new chance, after all.

The small house, two blocks away on Oak Street, proved to be everything the café wasn't. Made of sturdy red brick, it had gable eaves and a wide front porch. The eaves and the porch had recently been painted a bright white that matched the old-fashioned wicker chairs. Russet and gold chrysanthemums bloomed in redwood planters, and the lawn, which still bore a lingering tinge of green, had been recently mowed. A poinsettia, larger than any Hannah had ever seen, practically covered the entire south wall of the house; a few leaves had begun to turn scarlet.

"It's lovely," she said with a happy sigh. It was going to be all right, after all. She turned to her son. "How long has it been since you've seen a picket fence?"

"I've never seen a picket fence," Scott pointed out.

"Of course you haven't," Hannah murmured, still entranced by what seemed more an enchanted cottage than a proper house. "We had a picket fence around our yard when I was a little girl."

"In Cedar Falls?"

"In Cedar Falls," Hannah said. "I used to walk along the top rail and pretend I was a circus tightrope walker."

"Things must have been pretty boring in Iowa, huh, Mom?"

"I suppose it'd seem so now, but back then—"

"He's here," Scott interrupted, jumping up and down on the seat as he began fumbling with his seat belt.

"I suppose you're talking about Sheriff Murphy." Hannah glanced into her rearview mirror at the blue Jeep Cherokee that had pulled up behind them.

"Who else? Isn't he neat, Mom? A real sheriff." He was off, racing toward the Jeep.

Hannah watched Trace climb out of the truck and move toward the Volvo, his long stride exuding strength and power. "This is really very nice of you, Sheriff Murphy," she said as he approached.

"Would you do me a favor?" Trace asked.

"What kind of favor?"

So the lady was the cautious type. Which only made her decision to buy the Red Rock, sight unseen, all the more interesting. Trace decided Hannah Greene must have had one powerful reason for wanting to leave Connecticut.

"Would you mind calling me Trace? After twenty-five years of hearing my dad called Sheriff, and before that my grandfather, I'm having a little trouble getting used to the title."

"But not the duties," Hannah guessed.

His firm lips curved in a faint smile that showed in his eyes. "I suppose the work does come more naturally."

She wasn't really surprised by his admission. Trace Murphy possessed an unmistakable aura of confidence and self-control that reminded her unexpectedly of David, which in turn brought a stab of guilt for comparing her husband of nearly thirteen years with a virtual stranger.

"I thought that might be the case," she said quietly.

Trace watched the shadow come and go in her gray eyes and wondered at its cause. He'd just decided to turn the conversation onto a different, less personal tack, when the radio in the Jeep began to crackle.

"I've got a call," he apologized. "I'll be right back."

Mother and son stood on the tree-lined sidewalk and watched him walk back to the Jeep. The conversation was brief, over almost as soon as it had begun.

"I'm sorry to run out on you like this," Trace said as he returned, "but I'm afraid duty calls."

"I hope it's nothing dangerous."

"Just one of our good old boys causing a bit of trouble down at City Hall," he assured her. "I really am sorry to leave you in the lurch like this."

"Not exactly in the lurch," Hannah corrected as Dan drove up. Following him was Fred Wiley in a battered Chevy pickup, and bringing up the rear of the caravan was Cal Potter behind the wheel of the bright yellow pumper truck.

Trace gave her a slow, easy smile that was more dangerous than it should have been. "If you decide to give us a chance, Hannah, you'll discover New Chance can be a real friendly town."

"I'll keep that in mind."

He nodded. "You do that." He was halfway to the Jeep when he turned back toward her. "Oh, I almost forgot, I'll pick you and Scott up about six for dinner."

"Really, Sheriff—Trace," Hannah objected, ignoring the way Scott was yanking desperately on the back of her sweatshirt in an effort to influence her decision, "that isn't necessary."

"The Bar M is pretty remote, for a newcomer," Trace said. "What kind of sheriff would I be if I let you get lost your first day in New Chance?"

"But—"

The radio's insistent crackling began again. "Gotta go. See you this evening," he said over his shoulder as he began jogging toward the Jeep.

"Did I hear Trace say something about this evening?" Dan asked as he strolled toward Hannah with that same easy, loose-limbed stride that added to the undeniable attractiveness of his son.

"He offered to drive us to dinner," Hannah said. "I assured him that it really wasn't necessary. After all, I did manage to cross ten states coming here from Connecticut without getting lost, so I'm sure I could have found my way out to your ranch, but he insisted."

"Trace has always been a helpful boy," Dan said, rubbing his hand over his face to conceal a grin.

"Real helpful," Cal Potter agreed as he joined them.

Fred Wiley's choked sound was somewhere between a snort and a laugh.

Deciding to ignore their knowing looks, Hannah turned her attention to her son. "Come on, kiddo, let's go check out our new home."

Home. Was there a more wonderful word in the English language? Hannah wondered as she and Scott walked hand in hand toward the front door.

IF NEW CHANCE, ARIZONA brought to mind the neat little towns that had proliferated around the turn of the century, it was because the residents preferred to keep it that way. Located twenty-five miles from the interstate, it was the kind of town where shop owners still swept the sidewalks each morning, where there were more churches than movie theaters and summer Sundays in the park meant hot dogs, lemonade and baseball.

City Hall was located on Main Street, across from the town square, between the sheriff's office and the post office. The bronze plaque on the cornerstone revealed that the gray stone building was dedicated in 1904. In addition to the offices of the city council, the building housed various county, state and federal offices.

Trace had no sooner entered the building when a harried-looking man in his fifties, sporting a crew cut and wearing a brown, ill-fitting suit came marching toward him.

"It's about time you got here," Mel Skinner complained without preamble.

"Nice to see you, too, Mel," Trace said. "I came as soon as I got the call."

"Well, it wasn't soon enough," Skinner complained. "You'll never guess what the damn fool's threatening to do this time."

"You know I've never been much for guessing games," Trace said. "Why don't you just calm down and tell me why you took me away from helping one of New Chance's newest residents settle into her rental house?"

His news stopped Mel Skinner in his tracks, momentarily making the man forget about his own problems. "The widow's staying?"

"She's considering it."

"Does she know about this morning's fire?"

"She does."

"And she's still staying?"

"Looks as if she might."

The older man shook his head. "She's either crazy or a glutton for punishment."

"She didn't seem crazy." A paradox, perhaps. Her stoic reaction to the disaster that had awaited her had proved her strength. The confusion in her wide gray eyes as his gaze had settled on those enticing pink lips had hinted at a softness he'd like to explore further.

"Well, if she does decide to stay, she'll probably make it. Lord knows, she can't be any worse a cook than Johnny, and he's always done okay." Skinner decided. "Of course it doesn't hurt that the Red Rock is the only restaurant in town."

"That did tend to give Johnny a captive clientele," Trace agreed. "So, getting back to my reason for leaving a pretty young widow in the lurch—"

"Young?" Skinner interrupted. "Nobody said anything about her being young."

"Well, she is."

"How young?"

"Early thirties, I suppose. About Jake—"

"Pretty?"

Trace thought back to Hannah's shiny black hair, ca-
mellia-hued skin and gray eyes. "Pretty enough, I suppose," he said noncommittally. He had lived long enough
in New Chance to know that were he to tell the truth—that
he found her lovely—the rumor mill would have him head
over heels in love by lunchtime, engaged by dinner and
married before the week was out. "Now about Jake—"

"The damn drunken fool's threatening to take a baseball bat to the computer system!" Mel Skinner's Adam's
apple bobbed above the turquoise-and-silver slide of his
bolo tie. "You have to stop him, Trace. Without that computer, we might as well close up shop and go home."

"Perhaps that's what Jake has in mind," Trace suggested, making his way down the hallway to the Farm and
Home Administration offices on the first floor.

It wasn't the first time Jake Brennan's continuing feud
with the government had garnered official attention. Ever
since losing his land to government liens, Jake had been
waging an ongoing but futile war against the system. As
much as Trace felt for Jake, and all the other small land-
owners who'd gone under in the past few years, as sheriff
of Mingus County it was his job to maintain the peace.

"That computer is the property of the United States
Government," Skinner reminded him tartly. "If anything
happens to it, I'm going to hold you personally responsible."

The unmistakable sounds of Jake Brennan's swearing
filtered down the hall. "Why me?" Trace asked, hoping
that he'd be able to calm Jake down before things got out
of hand.

"Because you should have arrested him last week. When he threw that rock at my car."

"He missed."

"That's not the point. That just happens to be an official government car—do you have any idea how many forms I would have had to fill out if he'd put a dent in it, or even worse, broken a window?"

"Knowing the federal government, probably quite a few," Trace agreed, faintly amused.

"I want Brennan arrested, Trace. I don't care if he is your father-in-law, that's no excuse for favoritism."

Trace stopped in his tracks and looked down at the man. A dark storm threatened in his normally friendly eyes. "Favoritism is a pretty serious charge, Mel," he said quietly, folding his arms over his chest. "If I were you, I'd be sure of my facts before you began spreading that accusation all over town."

The challenge hummed in the air between the two men. "Just stop the damn fool from smashing my computer," Skinner said finally.

Trace nodded. "I'll do my best."

The scene that greeted him was not encouraging. A covey of secretaries hovered around the open door, staring into the office with a mixture of fascination and dismay. Papers had been ripped into shreds, the confetti-size pieces like fallen snow on the green tile floor. Color-coded files had been swept off desks, coffee cups along with them, leaving dark brown trails.

In the center of the chaos stood a small, wiry man wearing a green John Deere baseball cap, a red-and-gray plaid wool shirt, jeans and a pair of scuffed work boots. He was carrying a baseball bat—a Dave Winfield autographed Louisville Slugger, Trace noted irrelevantly.

"Morning, Jake." His voice was calm, steady.

From the way Jake Brennan's eyes narrowed suspiciously, it was obvious that he'd been expecting a harsher greeting. "Trace."

Trace pulled a bright red pack from his shirt pocket. "Want some gum?"

Brennan shook his head. His eyes remained watchful. Wary.

Trace shrugged. "Suit yourself." Taking a stick from the pack, he took a long time unwrapping it. "Nice day, isn't it?" He leaned back against a metal desk and crossed his legs at the ankles, frowning at the smudges of ash that still darkened the toes of his new boots. "Warm for the first week in November—more like Indian summer."

"Sheriff," Skinner interjected impatiently, "are you going to arrest this man or not?"

Trace ignored the bristling bureaucrat. "Of course the folks up at the ski bowl are probably biting their fingernails down to the quick, worrying whether they're going to get enough snow for a Thanksgiving weekend opening."

Brennan didn't answer, but his fingers relaxed imperceptibly on the bat.

"Looks like you've been busy," Trace said, glancing around the room.

"I came to get my land back," Jake Brennan growled. The sweet, pungent scent of whiskey floated on his breath.

"It isn't your land any longer," Mel Skinner said. "It belongs to the United States Government."

Brennan's answering oath was brief and harsh.

"Sheriff, I want this man arrested," Skinner insisted. "For disturbing the peace, destruction of official government property, not to mention assault and battery."

"Hell, I haven't assaulted anyone," Brennan shot back. "Leastwise not yet."

"And that's just how I'd like to keep it," Trace said quietly. "You know this isn't the way to handle things, Jake."

"You want to tell me what I should do? This squint-eyed little weasel steals my land—land that's been in the Brennan family for three generations—and I'm supposed to just lie down and take it?"

"That's it!" Mel Skinner slapped his hand down onto the desk. "I'm getting damned sick and tried of you telling anyone fool enough to listen to your alcoholic rantings that I'm a thief.... Trace, I want you to add libel to the rest of the charges."

"Mel," Trace drawled pleasantly, "I came here to do my job. Now if you don't leave this office right now, I'm afraid I'm going to have to take you in for obstructing justice."

"Obstructing justice?" Skinner asked disbelievingly. "What the hell does that mean?"

"It means you're getting in my way."

"You're also ticking me off," Brennan said, waving the bat and weaving drunkenly.

Skinner's angry gaze moved from Trace to Brennan to Trace again. "You're going to regret this, come election time."

Amused, Trace raised a brow. "Is that a threat, Mel?"

"Dammit," Brennan complained, "if you're gonna arrest me, Trace, do it now and get it over with. I'm tired of holding this thing up in the air." He'd begun to sway dangerously.

"You always did have a tendency to choke the bat," Trace agreed. "I've tried to tell you that an easy grip makes for a much smoother swing. Helps you hit those long balls." He held out his hand for the bat. "And since you brought it up, I suppose I don't have much choice but to take you in, Jake. Until you sober up."

Brennan's red-rimmed eyes shone with moisture. "He stole my land, Trace," he complained, dropping the white ash bat to his side. He didn't struggle as Trace relieved him of the weapon.

"We'll talk about it later, Jake," Trace promised soothingly. "For now, let's get you somewhere you can lie down. Before you fall down."

"He stole my land," Jake Brennan repeated to the small crowd gathered outside the office. "I made those payments. Damn bastard stole my ranch."

As the two men walked out to the Jeep together, Trace's arm around Jake's shoulder to steady him, tongues clucked and heads wagged. The confrontation was fast showing signs of replacing Mitzi Patterson and Dan Murphy as New Chance's hottest topic of conversation, but Trace knew that when people found out about the arrival of the enticing widow Greene, he and Jake would quickly become old news.

3

MITZI PATTERSON possessed the type of bubbly personality usually reserved for cheerleaders and Miss America contestants. Petite, blond and indefatigably good humored, she monopolized dinner conversation with humorous stories of other real-estate disasters she'd encountered over the years.

"When you saw that mess, I'll bet you wanted to make a big old U-turn and go right back to Connecticut," Mitzi said knowingly as Dan Murphy's housekeeper, a hefty Hispanic woman in her late sixties, cleared the dinner dishes.

The meal—a pale pastel swirl of squash soup with red pepper cream, succulent pink slices of grilled lamb and crunchy on the outside, steaming on the inside sweet potato fries—had been superbly prepared. Hannah made a note to compliment the woman before leaving.

"I considered it," Hannah answered, taking a sip of coffee. It was rich, dark and strong, laced with chocolate. She wondered fleetingly if the woman could be bribed into spinning her culinary magic at the Red Rock Café.

"And now?" A trio of gold bracelets jangled as Mitzi braced her elbows on the table and observed Hannah over linked fingers. Splinters of light from the wagon-wheel chandelier overhead were reflected in her bright blue contact lenses, making her steady look appear even more intent. Gone was the cheerleader, and in her place was a forty-eight-year-old real-estate saleswoman who, had she not chosen to live in New Chance, would have been perfectly at home pushing mansions in Beverly Hills.

Hannah shrugged carelessly, feigning uninterest. Before David's death, she'd been embarrassingly ignorant of the business world. The past eighteen months had been a painful but necessary crash course.

"I still haven't made up my mind what to do."

"Dan tells me that you've moved into the house."

"If you call unpacking a few clothes moving in," Hannah answered. She wasn't about to admit that she'd spent all day cleaning floors and polishing wood. There was no point in letting Mitzi know that she and Scott had already settled in.

"Renting a furnished house isn't that different from leasing an apartment for a vacation," she pointed out with a slight shrug. "We could be out in an hour, if we decide to go back to Connecticut."

"Is that the decision you're leaning toward?" If she was worried about losing a potential sale, Mitzi's friendly tone didn't reveal it.

Hannah took a sip of coffee and chose her words carefully. She could feel Scott's pleading gaze riveted on her face. Although it was extremely difficult, she managed to ignore him.

"I knew I'd have to do some work—redecorating, things like that," she answered finally.

Mitzi nodded her golden head approvingly. "Of course. With the exception of the new stove and hood, Johnny hasn't redecorated the Red Rock since Eisenhower was President. It's understandable that you'd want to put your own touches on the decor."

Personally, Hannah thought that referring to the faded linoleum and torn vinyl booths as decor was stretching a point, but opted not to argue. Not when more important things were at stake. "I'd probably have to gut the interior entirely and begin over again."

Mitzi didn't argue. There was no point. "At least the exterior's sound."

"Place has stood in the same spot for nearly one hundred years," Dan Murphy spoke up helpfully. "Since before statehood. Why, if those red rocks could talk..." He caught Mitzi's warning look. "You'd be buying yourself a heap of history," he finished up.

"Along with that new beginning you want so badly," Mitzi added sympathetically. She reached across the table and placed her hand on Hannah's. "Don't think I don't know how hard it is. Having to start all over again. I've been there, Hannah, and it's never easy. But it's worth it. In the long run."

Hannah thought of her plans for the Red Rock Café— stucco white walls, Navaho rugs on the floor, beamed ceilings, a bee-hive fireplace in the corner, the crackling warmth of the fire making the restaurant a cozy, attractive hideaway. It could work. If only...

"It'd take a lot of work," she murmured. "Not to mention money."

"Sure would. But you'd have a lot of willing workers," Dan reminded her.

"As for the money," Trace said, entering the conversation for the first time since it had turned to business, "I'm sure Johnny'd be willing to cut a few thousand off the purchase price. Wouldn't you say so, Mitzi?"

"Really, Trace," Hannah objected, "I'm perfectly capable of handling my own negotiations."

His bold smile was unabashedly unapologetic. "I never said you weren't, Hannah." He turned his attention back to Mitzi. "Well?"

"I'm sure I could convince him to see the wisdom of lowering the price," Mitzi agreed with a bright, professional smile. "Especially since the fire was his own fault. Not to mention the little matter of the insurance."

"I've no doubt that when you put your mind to it, you could convince a man to do just about anything, Mitzi," Trace said approvingly.

"I've always been a firm believer in not giving up, that's for sure." Mitzi's eyes cut quickly to Dan, then back to Hannah. "Johnny's the impatient sort and he is anxious to move to Bakersfield. I'm sure we can work out a deal agreeable to everyone involved."

"Then there's always the little matter of the sales commission," Trace said.

Mitzi paled ever so slightly. "Sales commission?"

"Seeing as how the entire town's willing to help Hannah salvage her restaurant, I figured you'd want to cut your commission in order to give her a bit more operating capital," Trace explained. "If you cut your commission, I'm sure Johnny'd be pleased to pass the additional savings on to Hannah."

"Him bein' so eager to move to Bakersfield and all," Dan tacked on.

Mitzi chewed on her bottom lip; and Hannah imagined the wheels turning inside the real-estate woman's head. "I suppose I could live with five percent," she said finally.

Two percent less than the seven Hannah knew Johnny had agreed to pay. The additional money could buy new dishes. As much as she resented Trace taking over what should have been her business, Hannah gave him an appreciative smile, only to discover he wasn't finished.

"Now, sweetheart," he objected with a slow, coaxing smile, "everyone in town knows that you expected to be sitting on that listing until way into the twenty-first century. Even at three percent, you'd still come out smelling like a rose."

"Why don't I just donate my entire commission," Mitzi complained.

"That'd be real hospitable of you," Trace said agreeably. "And I know Hannah would appreciate it. Wouldn't you?"

Entranced with the power of Trace's smile, Hannah took a moment to answer. "Of course I would, but—"

"Then it's settled." Trace rubbed his hands together with obvious satisfaction.

Hannah still couldn't believe it. "But surely you didn't mean that? About donating your commission?"

Mitzi shrugged her cashmere-clad shoulders, knowing defeat when it was staring her in the face. "Shoot, honey, it's almost the end of the year. If I make any more money, I'll just have to give most of it to the tax man."

It was too much. Hannah blinked, hoping that she could keep from embarrassing herself by breaking into tears. "I've heard about Western hospitality," she said, forcing her words past the lump in her throat, "but don't you think you're all taking this a bit too far?"

"Not at all," Dan insisted. "New Chance is a family town, Hannah. Always has been. We all know one another and more importantly, we care, whether we're dancing at our weddings or mourning our dead. We also understand that some people—city people mostly—might consider that old-fashioned. Even boring." He shrugged his wide shoulders. "But that's just the way we are."

Hannah didn't consider such behavior at all boring. Old-fashioned, perhaps, but nice. However, she'd heard about the way small towns tended to be standoffish with newcomers and wondered if Dan was taking too much for granted.

"I think it's a wonderful way to live," she said truthfully, "but don't forget, I'm new here."

"We don't force anyone to live in New Chance, Hannah," Trace said quietly. "People stay because they like what the town has to offer. If you decide to stay, you'll be one of us."

She still couldn't believe it could be that simple. "But—"

"One of these days you'll come to understand," Dan interjected with a reassuring smile. "But for now, why don't you just relax and enjoy dessert. Maria's chocolate walnut cake is famous in Mingus County. You could do worse than serve it at your new restaurant."

Her restaurant. A dream come true. All right, Hannah thought, perhaps right now her dream was a little sooty. And in need of some renovation. But in a few weeks the Red Rock Café would reopen and she'd be in business. Hannah laughed for the first time in months.

"Thank you," she said. "Thank you all."

Dan and Mitzi murmured a response. Trace didn't answer. He was too busy banking the slow fire that her throaty laugh had stirred.

"Does that mean we're staying?" Scott asked.

Hannah turned toward her son. He was practically bouncing up and down with unrestrained enthusiasm. "Yes. We're staying."

The heavy oak chair clattered on the floor as Scott jumped to his feet and threw his arms around Hannah's neck. "Everything's going to turn out just great, Mom," he promised. "Just you wait and see."

Returning her son's enthusiastic hug, Hannah felt Trace watching her. Looking up, her wary gaze collided with his openly interested one. Trace smiled, a slow, masculine smile that was every bit as sexy as it was dangerous. Telling herself that New Chance's sheriff was obviously no different from Greenwich's lascivious shrink when it came to women, Hannah decided that it was time to leave.

"We'd better get going," she said. "We're enrolling Scott in school tomorrow. He should be getting to bed."

"But Mom," Scott started to complain.

Hannah cut him off with a brisk wave of her hand. "I'm not hearing a word of argument, young man," she insisted firmly, turning to Dan and Mitzi. "Thank you very much for the meal and all your help."

"It was our pleasure," Dan said.

"Sure was," Mitzi agreed. "It'll be nice having a new friend to talk to. And shop with." A sudden thought lit up her eyes. "In fact, if you want, we can drive down to Phoenix and I can introduce you to another friend of mine. Pam's a decorator. You'd love her stuff."

"I think it's going to be some time before I can afford a decorator."

"I understand that, honey. But I was thinking more about using her professional discount to buy some material to recover those tacky booths. And maybe a few rugs for the floor."

Things were getting better and better. If it wasn't for the unnerving way Trace was looking at her....

"I'd appreciate that," Hannah said, steadfastly ignoring Trace as she returned Mitzi's smile. She turned to her son. "Come on, Scott. You've had a busy day and it's getting late."

"It's only eight o'clock," Scott pointed out. "And I'm not tired."

"Well, surely Trace would like to take us home so he can get on with whatever else he had planned for the evening."

She shot him a hopeful glance, but Trace proved no help whatsoever. He merely leaned back in his chair, studying her lazily. "I'm in no hurry to leave."

Hannah frowned. It had been a long day for her, too, and she was suddenly exhausted. But she was afraid that it was more than simple tiredness that had her feeling so tense.

"You have school tomorrow," she said, turning her attention back to her son.

"I had school in Connecticut, too. And I still never went to bed before nine o'clock."

Perhaps the son wasn't tired, Trace considered, but the mother was exhausted. Studying her more closely, he observed the faint lines of fatigue bracketing her mouth and the soft shadows under those incredible gray eyes. And as much as he would have been perfectly content to spend the remainder of the night watching her, listening to the lush sound of her voice, sympathy made him decide to help her out.

"Come on, Scott," he said suddenly, rising from his chair. "If you like, you can talk on the police radio on the ride home."

Disbelief and hope warred on Scott's face. Hope finally won out. "Really?"

Trace picked up his hat from the sideboard and plunked it down onto the boy's dark head. "Really."

The brim of the Stetson practically covered Scott's eyes. He pushed it back to look up at Trace with undisguised adoration. "Wow."

"But there's just one important rule."

"What rule?"

"You're not allowed to cuss. It's against regulations."

"I never cuss," Scott said, not quite truthfully. Hannah knew that he and Jimmy Walker had begun practicing their swearing just last month.

"I didn't, either, at your age," Trace lied with a laugh. Draping his arm over Scott's shoulder, he led him toward the front door, leaving Hannah to follow.

On the ride back to the house, Hannah was happy to sit in the back seat of the Jeep and watch her son practically burst with importance as he called in their destination to the deputy manning the base unit. When Cal Potter didn't seem surprised to hear the voice of an eight-year-old coming over the airwaves, Hannah wondered if everyone in town knew Trace had driven her out to his father's ranch this evening and decided that they probably did.

"I suppose Scotty and I have been provoking a great deal of speculation," she said softly, not wanting to wake her son, who'd finally fallen asleep.

Trace shrugged. "It's been all good, if you're worried."

"I wasn't exactly worried. Not really. It's just that . . ." Hannah's voice trailed off. She'd driven down from Albuquerque that morning, had been faced with the devastation at the Red Rock, had unpacked, cleaned up the house, and negotiated a real-estate deal, all in one day. Dead tired, her weary brain couldn't come up with the words necessary to properly explain her feelings.

"You're sick and tired of people speculating about your life. About whether you're not grieving long enough, or too long, or whether this idea of starting your own restaurant is a reasonable, thought-out decision or merely an overreaction to your situation. And you're especially fed up with everyone handing out advice and blithe platitudes, as if they were something that could ease your pain."

The depth of empathy, in a man she'd been ready to dismiss as just another drugstore cowboy, surprised Hannah. Their eyes met in the rearview mirror, and in the muted silver glow of moonlight she could see the compassion in his steady gaze. But there was understanding there as well.

"I suppose, as sheriff, you've witnessed a lot of pain."

"Too much." He returned his attention to the road. "But the observation came from personal experience, Hannah. Not professional."

She was curious, in spite of herself. "You're not married, are you?"

"No. Not at present."

"But you were?"

Trace waited for the pain, relieved when it didn't come. He'd thought himself over Ellen's death, but there was something about Hannah Greene, something about the feelings she inspired, that had left him strangely unsure of anything. The springtime scent of wild flowers that clung to her skin bloomed in the warmth of the Jeep's heater. His body ached; he ignored it.

"I was once. She died."

The night sky was lush black velvet, studded with diamonds, extending as far as the eye could see. They could have been the only people in the world. And in the dark, swirling quiet, Hannah was suddenly sorry she'd brought the subject up. It was too personal. Too intimate.

"I'm sorry." She regretted her words the moment they'd left her lips. It was the same thing everyone had said to her when they'd learned of David's death. Although well meant, the phrase sounded as empty to her now as it had eighteen months ago.

As if able to read her mind, Trace gave her a faint, reassuring smile in the rearview mirror. "So was I."

Hannah longed to ask how long ago his wife had died. And how. She would have been young; it must have been an accident. Or worse yet, some painful, lingering disease. At least David's death had been mercifully quick. She wondered how Trace had gone about putting his life back together. How he'd overcome the guilt and the anger at being the one left behind.

Hannah wanted to know all those things, but she refrained from asking, knowing that it was none of her business.

"It gets better," he said into the darkness.

She managed a slight, answering smile. "I know."

Trace nodded. "I figured you did."

That was all either one of them said until Trace pulled up in front of her redbrick house. Scott was sprawled on the front seat, the smile on his lips suggesting that he was reliving his moments as New Chance's assistant deputy.

"I'll carry him in for you," Trace offered.

"Thanks, but you don't have to bother. I can do it."

"It's no bother, Hannah," Trace insisted quietly. Firmly. Without giving her time to argue, he scooped the sleeping boy into his arms. "Lead the way."

Hannah wondered if Trace Murphy's refusal to hear a word of dissent was a result of his occupation or something in his nature. Whatever, he was going to have to learn that he couldn't run her life the way he ran New Chance. Not wanting to wake her sleeping son by arguing, she decided to let Trace get away with his presumptuous behavior for now. But if he thought such high-handed actions were going to be a normal occurrence, the man definitely had another think coming.

She'd already unpacked what few items she'd brought with her; the small house was neat and tidy. Books filled the built-in shelves, rag rugs brightened the floor and lush

green plants that she'd babied along all the way from
Connecticut bloomed vigorously atop polished table-
tops. The air was fresh and clean and smelled of lemons.

"You've gotten a lot done."

"I didn't want Scott living out of boxes any longer than
necessary. Children need a great deal of stability, although lord knows the poor kid hasn't had a lot of it
lately," she said with a little sigh. Realizing that she was in
danger of sounding sorry for herself, Hannah drew in a
deep breath. "His bedroom is right down this hall," she
said. "It's the second door on the left."

Her brisk manner would have convinced Trace that he'd
imagined her momentary lapse of control had it not been
for the lingering sadness in her voice. He followed her
down the hall. She was wearing a rose-colored sweater, a
dark gray skirt that fell to mid-calf and a pair of pewter-
gray boots with high heels that contributed to a slight sway
in her walk he found irresistible.

She led him into what was definitely a boy's room.
Posters of baseball and football superstars covered the
walls. Model cars and plastic action figures filled the blue
painted wooden shelves beside the window and comic
books describing the exploits of invincible superheroes
were strewn over the floor.

Scott remained dead to the world as Hannah whipped
the Star Wars bedspread away, permitting Trace to lay the
sleeping child down on the mattress. He stood in the
doorway and watched as Hannah changed her son out of
his jeans and sweatshirt into a pair of pajamas bearing the
names and logos of popular NFL teams. He decided
motherhood suited her. She was soft and incredibly gentle,
but from what he'd witnessed thus far, the lady was definitely no pushover. Hannah Greene was, to borrow from

his grandfather's vernacular, one plucky little lady. Scott was a very fortunate little boy.

"I'd offer you a cup of coffee," she said, once they returned to the living room, "but I'm afraid that's something else I forgot to buy when I went to the market this afternoon."

"That's okay. I should be going anyway. You look as if you need to get to bed."

She lifted a hand to her hair. No longer tied back with this morning's ribbon, it fell in a sleek dark curtain that curved beneath her chin. "That bad, huh?" The fleeting glimpse of vulnerability in her eyes tugged at something inside him.

"Not at all." He smiled, restraining the impulse to touch her face, to see if the skin that covered those high cheekbones was as soft as it looked. "Actually, I've been wanting to tell you all evening how lovely you looked, but I was afraid you'd get spooked and bolt."

With apparent calm, Hannah met his approving gaze. "I'm not that easily spooked."

"I'm beginning to realize that. How about if I tell you that you smell terrific?"

They were face-to-face, their bodies close. Trace watched mild surprise appear in her eyes. Surprise and a vague hint of passion that made him wonder exactly how long the lady had been a widow.

It took a Herculean effort, but Hannah kept her voice steady. "Since that scent is the single remaining indulgence I allow myself these days, I'd say thank you."

"You're welcome." When the urge to touch her became irresistible, Trace slipped his hands into his pockets. "You know," he said, looking around the room, "from all the work you've put into the house, it's obvious that you'd already decided to stay in New Chance before I picked you and Scott up this evening."

"It wasn't as if I had many other options."

"Nevertheless, now that I know you intended all along to stay, I'm doubly impressed with how you handled Mitzi. Inside that cotton-candy exterior dwells the predatory business instincts of an old-time robber baron. You must be a natural-born businesswoman, to be able to bluff like you did."

"Hardly." His warm, appreciative gaze was making her pulse jerky. "When it comes to business, eighteen months ago I was a mere babe in the woods."

Eighteen months was a long time. Trace wondered if it was long enough. "But fate provided you with a crash course."

"That's one way of putting it."

Faint frown lines had formed between her dark brows. His fingers practically itched with the desire to reach out and rub them away. "Well, you obviously passed with flying colors." The mantel clock chimed nine, reminding Trace that Hannah had already had a very long and tiring day. "I'd better get going," he said. "Merlin tends to get testy if I don't get back on time."

"Is Merlin one of your deputies?"

"He's my dog." He stopped in the doorway. "Oh, by the way, Hannah, in case you're concerned about the success of your restaurant, you can stop worrying. It's going to be a smash."

It was her smile—slow, warm, enticing—that did it. Unable to resist any longer, he ran a finger along her jawline. It was just as he'd suspected—ivory satin. "I'm glad you decided to stay, Hannah."

His butterfly-soft touch shouldn't feel so good, she thought. Such a delicate, harmless caress shouldn't make her body hum. But it did.

"I'm glad, too," she said in a voice that was little more than a whisper as she backed away—both physically and emotionally—from his provocative touch. "Thank you for all your help."

Trace saw the emotions swirling in her eyes. There was desire there, unwilling though it might be, but it was the unmistakable wariness that captured his attention. He was experienced enough to know that if he pushed now, he'd only end up chasing her away. There was plenty of time, Trace reminded himself. The lady wasn't going anywhere.

"No problem," he said with a careless shrug. "After all, it's—"

"Part of the job."

Her soft voice sounded disappointed. Afraid she'd think he was laughing at her, Trace withheld the victorious smile her regretful little tone encouraged.

"Not at all," he corrected amiably. "Actually, in your case, Hannah, it was definitely one of the perks."

He said good night, inclined his head briefly, then turned away, leaving her to watch as he walked unhurriedly toward the Jeep. She was still standing in the doorway, bathed in the spreading amber glow of the porch light, when he pulled away from the curb.

Once he'd turned the corner, out of Hannah's sight, Trace threw back his head and laughed all the way to the station. He couldn't remember the last time he'd felt this good.

4

TO HANNAH'S SURPRISE and relief, the following days passed smoothly. She enrolled Scott in school, and with the fortunate ability her son had to adapt to new situations and new people, he'd made several new friends by lunchtime on the first day and spent each evening regaling her with tales of life in the third grade.

Even beginning the renovation of the Red Rock Café turned out to be less of a problem than she'd expected. True to their word, Cal Potter, Fred Wiley and Dan Murphy had shown up at eight o'clock that first morning and worked through the day, stopping only for the sandwiches Hannah had insisted on bringing from home.

Cal's assertion that he was handy with a hammer and nails proved to be an understatement. He and his brother Hal moved walls, began rewiring the restaurant for additional overhead lighting and made plans to replace the kitchen countertops with gleaming ceramic tile and smooth marble slabs designed for rolling out pie crusts and kneading bread. Although she was no carpenter, Hannah worked right along with the men, happy to do whatever menial tasks they assigned her.

ONE WEEK after work had begun on the restaurant, Trace put in an appearance. Hannah was alone, sanding peeling paint from the kitchen walls when he walked in unannounced. Engrossed in her task, she wasn't immediately aware of his presence, which allowed him to observe her undetected.

She was standing on the second rung of a ladder, her back to him as she vigorously sanded the smoke-darkened wall. Watching the snug jeans pull even tighter as she leaned over to concentrate on a particularly troublesome spot, Trace experienced a sharp, physical tug.

"The view around this place has definitely improved," he said.

At the sound of his voice, Hannah froze, a million scattered thoughts flashing through her mind, the first of which was that she shouldn't be so pleased he'd finally decided to make an appearance. The second, third, fourth and millionth were that she looked a mess. Forcing herself to relax—neck, shoulders, arms—she glanced back over her shoulder.

"If you've dropped in for lunch, I'm afraid you're a little premature. We're not quite open."

"So I see." He glanced around the kitchen, which looked as if it had recently been the battleground for World War III. "Looks as if you and the boys have been busy."

Hannah laughed. "Goodness, Sheriff, are you always so tactful? In the past week, working nearly around the clock, we have managed to turn an unholy mess into a world-class disaster." Humorous pride danced in her eyes as she took in the scene. "Believe it or not, there is order in this chaos."

"I figured any woman as organized as you are would have a plan."

She climbed down the ladder, meeting him halfway in the center of the room. "Oh? Where did you get that little insight?"

Her face, which was even more exquisite than he remembered, was free of makeup. Although her flawless skin was porcelain-pale, her lips had a soft pink tinge that made him wonder if they'd taste as sweet as they looked.

"Uh . . . Scott."

"I've been meaning to talk to you about Scott stopping by the station every day on his way home from school," she said. "He assured me that you don't mind, but—"

Trace waved off her objection. "Don't worry about it. I really like having him visit. He's a great kid, Hannah. Bright, inquisitive, polite. You should be proud."

He couldn't have said anything that would have pleased her more. "I suppose I am."

"Good. Then you won't be upset when I tell you that he filled me in on all your secrets."

She certainly hoped that wasn't true. As it was, Hannah knew that were she to be perfectly honest with herself, she'd have to admit that she'd been all too aware of Trace Murphy's absence. "Secrets?"

"Secrets," he confirmed. "Such as your vast organization skills. I'm in the process of trying to clean out the files down at the office and it's driving me insane. Your son assured me that you could straighten both me and my files out in no time." His green eyes narrowed. "He also says you make lists."

"I do."

"Really?" He made it sound like a character flaw.

"Would it make you feel better to know that I always lose the lists right after making them?"

"Immensely."

Trace's answering grin warmed Hannah to the core. She decided that if they could find some way to harness the power of that rakish smile, she'd save herself an enormous power bill every month.

"Perfect people are intimidating," he added.

"I can't imagine you being intimidated by anyone. Or anything."

Again that devastating smile. "It's the badge—gives people the wrong image. Actually, if you want to know the truth, gorgeous, sexy women have always intimidated me."

"Then you should feel completely comfortable around me." Damn. From the way that sounded, Trace was bound to think she was fishing for compliments. Which she wasn't, Hannah assured herself. Not really.

"Funny you should mention that," he murmured. "As it happens, I've been giving the matter a great deal of thought lately."

He rubbed his jaw as he studied her, his leisurely inventory missing nothing, from the top of her sleek dark head down to her worn running shoes. Hannah had a sudden urge to smooth the wrinkles from her New York Giants sweatshirt. An urge she managed, with effort, to resist.

"Well?" she asked finally, when she could not stand his silent scrutiny another minute.

He didn't answer immediately. Instead, he approached within inches of her suddenly tense body. "I have been thinking about you, Hannah."

"Oh, really?"

"Really." His thumb traced the curve of her upper lip, leaving a scattering of sparks on her skin. "Probably too much, if you want to know the truth. Have you thought abuot me?"

"No." Her voice was calm; she was not.

Trace laughed softly. Hannah's heartbeat quickened. "It's a good thing you're not under oath. I'd have to run you in for perjury."

"Do you always arrest women who resist your advances, Sheriff?"

"I never have, but now that you bring it up, I'll keep it in mind," he said amiably. "Would you accuse me of police harassment if I were to kiss you, Hannah?"

She was going to kiss him because she wanted to, Hannah assured herself. Not because of the way the feel of his thumb on her skin and the warmth of his gaze was making her knees weak. "I suppose that would depend on what type of kiss it was."

He smiled. "Why don't we try it and find out?" He lowered his head, watching her eyes close just before he touched his lips to hers.

Hannah sighed her pleasure as his breath whispered over her skin. His lips, as they moved on hers, were clever, experienced, but that was not a surprise. Hannah knew that a man as good-looking as Trace would have had plenty of opportunity to perfect his technique. What was a surprise was that such an impossibly light touch could kindle such scintillating heat.

A warm, golden mist surrounded her, luring her deeper and deeper as he deepened the kiss, degree by glorious degree. His mouth was firm, persuasive, his lips nibbling, teasing at hers, coaxing a response. His broad hand cupped the back of her neck, holding her still, but Hannah could not have moved if she wanted to. Which she didn't. Something stirred deep inside her. Something she'd thought had died with David. Arousal. Need.

Desires too long untapped rose to the surface; mindless pleasure clouded her mind, drawing her into a world of steamy, potent sensations. She could get lost in this dark and smoky world, Hannah realized as his tongue brushed lightly over her lips, then retreated, tempting hers to follow suit. Too easily.

Trace knew the kiss, which had begun as a casual sort of experimentation, was turning out to be something far more intense, more dangerous. Almost profound. The attraction had been there from the beginning, along with an impulsive masculine desire that he refused to apologize for. But attraction had never made his head spin the way it was spinning now. And desire had never made him feel as if he were slowly, inexorably sinking into quicksand.

He fought the need to crush her to him as he controlled the urge to drag her to the worn linoleum underfoot and quench the fire that was raging through him. With hands that were no longer steady, he released her, while he still could.

Both Hannah and Trace were shaken; both were determined to not to reveal it. Bending down, Hannah picked up the Stetson that had fallen to the floor. When she was certain that she could do so calmly, she met his eyes.

"Well," she said, "that was . . ."

"Something else to think about," he finished for her.

God, she was lovely! Lingering passion swirled in her eyes and her lips. He could still taste those warm, pliant lips, blushed a deep rose from the heated kiss. In that fleeting moment, as their eyes met, Trace promised himself that he and Hannah were going to make love. But, he decided, seeing the wariness that was fast replacing the desire in her gaze, he was willing to wait. Perhaps the wait would do them both some good.

"Believe it or not, I came here today on official business."

Her head was still spinning and her legs felt numb from the knees down. As she leaned against the counter for support, Hannah decided that her best defense would be to treat the devastating kiss lightly. She crossed her arms over her chest. "Tell me, Sheriff, is kissing newcomers to New Chance part of your job?"

Trace winked as he took his time putting his hat back on. "I don't suppose you'd believe I'm the Welcome Wagon representative."

"No, I wouldn't."

"I didn't think so." He reached into a pocket, pulling out a piece of folded paper. "The city council met last night and asked me to drop this by."

Hannah took the offered paper, scanning the lines of type. "It's a contract?"

"With the town, to provide meals for the jail," he agreed. "Johnny always had a verbal agreement, but we've got a new mayor, George Masterson, owner of Masterson's Mercantile, who's gung ho enough to want everything in writing. The price is the same as Johnny's been getting for the past three years, but if it's not enough, feel free to negotiate. As you can probably tell from the way he fell behind on his insurance payments, Johnny was a miserable businessman."

"The price is fair," she murmured, studying the brief document. "How many prisoners are we talking about?"

"Not that many," he assured her. "Probably two or three a month, and most of them are merely guys who've had a bit too much to drink on Saturday night. They're usually gone by Sunday lunchtime, so we're not talking about anything that's going to take time away from your work at the restaurant. Or make you any money," he said somewhat apologetically.

"Well, I guess this makes it official," she said, signing the paper before handing it back to him. "I'm now a bona fide resident of New Chance."

He took the paper without looking at it. "You've no idea how happy that makes me." Reaching out, Trace gathered her dark hair in his hand, drawing her to him with a gentle tug.

"Really, Sheriff," Hannah objected, "for a man who came here today on official business, your behavior isn't very businesslike."

"We've already gotten the business part of this conversation out of the way. And for the record, Hannah, that kiss was entirely personal. You might want to keep that in mind next time."

The hint of amusement in his tone made her defiantly lift her chin. "What makes you think there's going to be a next time?"

"If I didn't think there was going to be a next time, my sweet, fragrant Hannah, I wouldn't be so willing to leave things unfinished this time." He brushed his lips teasingly against her frowning mouth, creating a flare of heat. "I'll be seeing you."

As he left the kitchen, Hannah tried to decide whether to take Trace's closing words as a promise, or a threat.

THE WORK CONTINUED practically nonstop for seven days. Days in which Hannah spent more time than she would have liked thinking about Trace. Despite orders to the contrary, her rebellious mind continued to recall the kiss she'd shared with him in riveting, sensual detail. Scott was no help at all as he continued to regale her with stories of life around the sheriff's office. One week after Trace's unexpected visit to the restaurant, her son returned home with a law-enforcement recruiting poster.

"It's really neat, isn't it, Mom?" Scott asked that evening, for the umpteenth time.

The poster depicted a scrubbed and polished young man in a starched khaki uniform standing beside a patrol car, looking for all the world like the last bastion between the bad guys and the general public. Bearing the title Exploring Law Enforcement, it had been assigned the spot of

honor on Scott's bedroom wall, between Yankee greats
Don Mattingly and Ricky Henderson.

"Neat."

Hannah pressed the ground chuck between her hands,
forming it into patties. Although cheeseburgers were not
exactly haute cuisine, they were her son's favorite. They
were also fast, which would enable her to put in four or
five more hours at the café after dinner.

For the past two weeks, she'd worked out a schedule
where Scott would come down to the café in the afternoon and do his homework while she worked. They'd
both return to the house for dinner and conversation at six.
At seven, Mrs. MacGregor, who lived across the street,
would arrive to stay with Scott while Hannah went back
to the Red Rock until around midnight, after which she'd
return home with her bones aching and muscles protest-
ing.

After a too-brief hot bath, she'd spend at least another
hour poring over her accounts, searching for ways to turn
red ink to black. It was during those lonely, dark hours
that Hannah found herself wishing for a fairy godmother
who'd sweep in, wave her magic wand, mutter some gib-
berish and whisk her away to an enchanted tropical island.
Or at least tell her a way to cut ten percent off the plumbing costs. When the fairy godmother failed to make an
appearance, she'd fall into bed, where it would seem as if
she'd no sooner get to sleep than the alarm would go off
and it would be time to begin the process all over again.

"Warren offered me all his He-Man figures for my
poster," he divulged. Warren, the nine-year-old who lived
next door, had become what Scott described as his sec-
ond-best friend. Trace, not surprisingly, occupied top position. "But I told him I wouldn't trade for anything."

"I hope you thanked Trace."

"Sure, what kind of kid do you think you raised?" he complained with a grin.

Hannah returned the smile. "A terrific kid."

"I think you're terrific, too," Scott said as he went to the refrigerator. "Can I have a soda?"

"You know it's milk with dinner."

"Trace lets me have soda," Scott revealed as he poured the milk into a tall glass emblazoned with cartoon figures.

"He does?"

"Yeah. But only because I told him you sometimes let me have it," he said quickly. "That's okay, isn't it?"

Knowing that her son was afraid she'd ban further visits to his newfound hero, Hannah kept the conversation light. "So long as you don't spoil your dinner."

Scott climbed up on the bar stool and watched as she turned on the burner. "I won't. Can we invite Trace to dinner sometime?"

"I suppose. Sometime," she answered vaguely, having no intention of chasing after a man who'd obviously already lost interest. After the heated kiss they'd shared, Hannah had been expecting Trace to visit the café. When he failed to put in an appearance, she could only assume he'd moved on to greener—and easier—pastures.

"When?"

"I don't know, honey. Trace is a very busy man."

"But he doesn't work nights unless there's an emergency. He told me."

"Still, he undoubtedly has his own plans."

"No, he doesn't. Most nights he and Merlin just eat frozen dinners."

"I take it you've met Merlin," Hannah said, grating the block of cheddar cheese onto a plate.

"Yeah." Scott reached out and picked up some cheese, popping it into his mouth. "He mostly hangs around the sheriff's office. He's really neat. Can we get a dog, Mom? There's plenty of room in the backyard."

"I don't know, Scott. A dog might get lonely, with you at school all day and me at work."

"I could take him to play with Merlin."

"I don't think a law-enforcement agency is any place for boys and dogs to be playing."

"But—"

"Let me think about it," Hannah said, interrupting what she knew was going to be a long drawn-out plea.

"Sure." He plucked some more cheese from the growing pyramid. "You know," he suggested guilelessly, "maybe if you came down to Trace's office and meet Merlin, and saw what a neat dog he is . . ."

Hannah held up her hand warningly. "I said, let me think about it."

The doorbell rang before Scott could answer. "I'll get it," he said, sliding off the stool. He was out of the room in a flash, and a moment later Hannah heard the low murmur of voices, one youthful, one deep and compelling.

She instinctively lifted a hand to her hair, remembering the meat on her palm just in time.

"Hey, Mom," Scott called out as he ran into the room, "Look what Trace brought me!" He held up a sheet of paper, looking as if he'd just been given the keys to his own private toy store. "Fingerprints. From a real live bank robber."

At least the man had original taste in gifts, Hannah thought. She hadn't seen Scott that excited since . . . Actually, she wasn't certain she'd ever seen him that excited.

"Hello, Sheriff," she said with measured calm as Trace strolled into her kitchen carrying a brown paper bag. "What can I do for you?"

"I've come for dinner."

"Dinner?" Hannah glanced over at her son, who was busy matching his own fingertips to the smudged ink stains.

Picking up on the situation, Trace turned toward Scott as well. "I thought you said your mother wanted me to come over for dinner."

"She did," the boy insisted. "Didn't you, Mom?"

"I believe my exact words were 'perhaps sometime'," Hannah corrected.

Scott's anxious, coaxing gaze went back and forth between his mother and his friend. "Well, this is sometime," he pointed out. "I think I'll go next door and show my fingerprints to Warren. He'll be really jealous." He escaped through the kitchen door before Hannah had a chance to object.

"You have exactly fifteen minutes," she called out to his back. "If you're not back by then, your burger will end up in a doggie bag for Merlin."

Trace chuckled. "I think that kid has a great future as a politician."

"If he lives that long," Hannah muttered. She was wearing an oversize scarlet sweater and those same snug jeans that made him wonder why he'd stayed away so long.

"I can go," he offered. He'd stayed away, despite an almost overwhelming ache to see her—to touch her—in order to allow Hannah time to adjust to the idea of a new man in her life. When Scott had asked him to dinner this afternoon, he'd mistakenly assumed that the invitation had come from the mother, not the boy.

"You're welcome to stay, if you don't mind cheeseburgers and fries," she said with forced casualness.

"Love 'em. Need any help?"

"I think I've got everything under control."

He certainly couldn't argue with that. If she were any more composed, Trace would begin to think he'd imagined that heated kiss they'd shared.

"I brought some wine," he offered, pulling the bottle out of the bag. Not trusting Fred Masterson's inventory of jug wine, Trace had driven the twenty miles to a wine and cheese shop in Sedona. The proprietor of the Cork and Cleaver had assured him that Hannah would approve of the vintage cabernet sauvignon.

Hannah's eyebrows rose as she studied the label. "Goodness, I feel as if I should dump the hamburgers in the disposal and whip up some fillet of beef *Périgourdine*."

"Does that mean I did okay?"

"Better than okay. But you needn't have spent so much money."

Trace shrugged. "It wasn't that much." Actually, he'd been stunned by the price, but had immediately decided Hannah was worth every dollar. "Do you have a corkscrew?"

"In the top right-hand drawer, next to the refrigerator. And don't forget, I'm in the business—I know how expensive that vintage is."

"Hey, lady, for your information, this happens to be my favorite drink with hamburgers."

She studied him curiously for a moment, then went back to forming a third hamburger patty. "Well, you certainly needn't have bothered on my account."

"I didn't," he lied blithely as he uncorked the wine. "Glasses?"

"In the cupboard to the left of the sink."

Trace found the glasses and was prepared to pour the ruby wine into them when something from a James Bond movie he'd once seen popped into his mind. "I suppose we should let this breathe for a while."

"I suppose so," Hannah agreed. "Not that I'd be able to tell the difference."

"You're kidding."

"Not at all. Although I really did try, I never managed to develop a discriminating wine palate."

"I would have figured a fancy Eastern chef such as yourself would be a real wine connoisseur."

"Don't tell anyone, but my teachers used to call me the class Philistine."

"Teachers?" Deciding that the wine had breathed long enough, Trace poured it into the stemmed glasses.

"At the New York Restaurant School."

"That's where you learned to cook?"

"Among other things. We studied everything from boiling eggs to restaurant design. The final thesis is a restaurant proposal including everything from menus and tableware to financing and negotiating your way through New York City's building codes."

"No wonder Mitzi was no match for you."

His admiration was somehow even more disconcerting than his earlier desire. Hannah shrugged off his compliment. "I suppose I did learn a lot about financing. Even if I did nearly flunk wine."

"That's good to know. Next time I'll stick to Ripple. Or better yet, Fred carries a Muscatel at the Mercantile that's just one step above antifreeze."

"What year?"

"Last week. And I have it on good authority that it's spent all that time aging in aluminum barrels."

She laughed. "I think even I could spot that. Do you really want to help?"

"I never say anything I don't mean, Hannah." He was smiling, but his eyes were discomfitingly grave.

Her throat went suddenly dry. She swallowed. "You can peel those potatoes. That is, if you wouldn't mind."

"You're in luck," Trace said as he picked one up. "Peeling's one of my few culinary skills. That and taking the aluminum foil off the top of TV-dinner trays."

"You're certainly fast," Hannah murmured, momentarily transfixed by the smooth, quick motion of his hands as he covered the bottom of the stainless-steel sink with curling brown potato skins.

"I peeled mountains of potatoes my first six months in the marines. The trick is to think of it as whittling."

"You were in the marines?" She plugged in the deep fryer after filling it with cooking oil.

"For eight years."

"What did you do?" she asked as she put the hamburgers under the broiler.

"I was an M.P." At her momentarily blank look, he explained, "Military Police."

"Did you become sheriff once you'd left the marines?"

"No. I spent three years working for the Phoenix P.D. Then Dad had his heart attack, so I came back and finished up his term as sheriff. The following year I was elected to the job and I figure I'll probably stick around until they vote me out."

If the glowing descriptions she'd been hearing about Trace for the past two weeks were any indication, Hannah decided he'd probably continue being sheriff of New Chance for as long as he lived.

"Do you miss the city?"

"Not at all. Actually, I'd been thinking about coming home for a long time. Dad's heart attack simply helped me to make my mind up a little sooner."

She wondered if he'd been married then, but didn't quite know how to ask without making the conversation too personal. "I would think being a city policeman would be exciting."

Trace shrugged as he dumped the raw potatoes into the stainless-steel basket. "Sometimes." They sizzled as he lowered the basket into the hot grease. "Although it's not at all like on TV, where the good guys have exactly sixty minutes, minus commercials, to catch the bad guys and get them put behind bars. Mostly it's boring detail work. Patrolling the streets, stuff like that."

"Don't tell Scott it's boring. He'd be heartbroken. Is being sheriff that much more exciting?"

"Actually, if you want to know the truth, Mingus County's pretty peaceful. As a general rule, being sheriff is about as exciting as watching two guys fish."

Hannah pulled the pan holding the burgers out from under the broiler and turned them. "Then why do you do it?"

"I think it was predestined. My great-grandfather was the first sheriff of New Chance. He was followed by my grandfather, then my father, now me. The potatoes are ready. Want me to set the table?"

"There are paper napkins in that cupboard to your right. The plates are on the shelf above them. Is that the only reason? Predestination?" From what she'd seen of Trace Murphy, Hannah would have expected the man to take a more active role in the planning of his life.

"Not really." To Hannah's surprise, he appeared almost embarrassed by her question.

"Well?" Her tone, while soft, invited elaboration.

"It'll sound corny," he warned.

"Corny?"

"Like something from an old John Wayne movie. You know, all that red-white-and-blue stuff about honor and integrity."

"I've always liked John Wayne movies. And there's certainly a great deal to be said for honor and integrity."

Trace stared at her for a full ten seconds. Finally, he took a deep breath and shook his head. "Okay, but don't say I didn't warn you.... I came home because I'm old-fashioned enough to feel as if I might actually be able to make a difference in people's lives."

"And you couldn't make a difference in Phoenix?"

"I might have, from time to time. But things are so big there, the system was too impersonal for my tastes. How about you?"

"Me?"

"What made you give up the big-city lights of Manhattan for the sleepy ambience of New Chance, Arizona?"

How could she explain that she'd based a major life-decision on something as whimsical as a town's name? Hedging the issue, she pulled aside the sunshine-yellow curtains and looked out the kitchen window.

"I wonder if I should call Scott. Dinner's nearly ready and he's still not home."

"He's still got a couple of minutes," Trace pointed out. "Conversation getting a little too personal again, Hannah?"

"Not at all," she insisted, taking the pan out from under the flame long enough to pile cheese on top of the burgers. "It was merely a question of the most return on my dollar. I couldn't afford to buy '21' or Lutèce, but I could afford the Red Rock Café."

Trace refilled their wineglasses and asked the question he'd been asking himself ever since meeting Hannah. "Surely there were other restaurants between here and New York you could afford to buy. Why this one? And why sight unseen?"

"The cheese is bubbling," she complained, pulling the broiler pan from the oven. "Where is he?"

Scott chose that moment to burst in the door. His face was flushed from the brisk November air. "Dumb ole Warren doesn't believe these are a real crook's fingerprints," he complained, tossing his jacket onto the back of a chair, where it slid down onto the floor.

"Pick up your jacket and hang it properly on the rack," Hannah instructed. "Then wash your hands and sit down to dinner before the hamburgers get cold."

"But what about Warren?"

"Warren can get his own dinner. I only made three burgers. Wash."

Recognizing the no-nonsense tone, Scott scooped up the denim jacket, tossed it onto the brass coatrack and went over to the sink where he pumped liquid soap onto his palms and waved them briefly under the water before wiping his hands on his jeans.

"They really are a crook's prints, huh, Trace?"

"Sure are. Big Bill Barkley was one of the most infamous bank robbers in Arizona."

"Is it all right for Scott to have them?" Hannah asked as she brought the cheeseburgers to the table.

"We were cleaning out the files," Trace assured her. "If I hadn't given them to Scott, I probably would have ended up throwing them away."

"Surely you need them for your records. Aren't they important evidence?"

Her tone was so sober, her look so sweetly grave, it was all Trace could do not to bend down and kiss her now, while her hands were filled with plates and she couldn't push him away. Knowing that Scott was nearby, he merely smiled.

"Hannah, Big Bill Barkley escaped from the Arizona State prison in 1925, after which time he was rumored to be hiding out with Butch Cassidy in Utah. I doubt there'll be any immediate need for his fingerprint file."

Scott frowned as he bit into his cheeseburger. "But Butch Cassidy died in Argentina," he said when he'd finished chewing. "With the Sundance Kid. I've seen the movie on cable, lots of times."

"That's what they say," Trace agreed. "However, his sister, Lula Parker, insisted that the men killed in Argentina were intentionally misidentified by a friend of Butch's to give Butch a chance to bury his past and go straight."

"Wow! Just think, Mom, my fingerprints belong to a friend of Butch Cassidy's."

"Just what every boy needs," Hannah said dryly, "a convict hero. . . . Do you actually believe that story?" she asked Trace.

"I don't really know. My grandfather believed it, but he had a crush on Lula back in those days, so he'd probably buy anything the lady said."

"Wow." Scott was awestruck. "Now I know what I'm going to write my English paper on. Can you help me, Trace?"

"I'd love to, sport, but Dad would be able to give you a lot more facts, since most of what I know is just rumor and passed-down family stories."

Scott mulled it over while he chewed on a catsup-soaked french fry. "Okay," he decided. "Mrs. Wilson said the papers have to be nonfiction. That's the truth, not made up," he elaborated for Hannah's benefit. "So I guess facts would be better. But the stories are great, too," he added, as if afraid of hurting Trace's feelings.

Amused, Trace winked. "Glad you like them. How about after we help your mom with the dishes, you and I go next door to Warren's and I'll verify your fingerprints."

"Gee," Scott said happily, "this is turning out to be a great night!"

5

"IT'S BEEN a nice evening," Hannah said a few hours later.
Scott, his reputation and fingerprints vindicated, had gone
to bed, leaving her alone with Trace. It had begun to rain,
a gentle autumn rain that sounded a steady tattoo on the
roof and contributed to the intimacy of the comfortably
furnished room.

"You sound surprised."

"I suppose I am," she admitted. She wouldn't have
thought she could feel so at ease in Trace Murphy's company. "Mrs. MacGregor certainly didn't seem surprised
when I called to tell her not to bother coming over this
evening."

"That may have something to do with the Mingus
County Sheriff's Department Jeep parked in front of your
house," he suggested.

"Probably." Hannah sighed. "By tomorrow it'll be all
over town that we had dinner together."

"Does that bother you?"

She shrugged. "I suppose not."

But it did. Trace could tell. Knowing that it took time
to get used to the fishbowl existence that was part and
parcel of life in New Chance, he sought to put her mind at
rest.

"I can tell everyone that I was testing out the cook," he
said helpfully. "So they'll know what they're getting into
when the Red Rock reopens."

"Just don't tell them I fed you cheeseburgers."

"Hey, don't knock cheeseburgers. They're considered gourmet fare around these parts."

His winning smile encouraged one in return, and as the evening went on, Hannah began to relax. In fact, it was as if a dam had burst as she told him of the continuing transformation of the Red Rock Café, from the newly plastered walls to the ceramic tile to the skylight Cal Potter had put in the entryway.

"You'd be amazed at the amount of light it lets in, even on cloudy days," she said, her face glowing with enthusiasm. "It makes the entry look so much larger. I'm thinking of getting a tree, nothing too big, maybe just a ficus, or bamboo, although bamboo might be too oriental for the southwestern fare I plan to serve. A banana tree would be wonderful, but they grow so large. And they need a lot of humidity. Perhaps I ought to stick with ficus."

"I've found that it's usually best to go with your first impulse," Trace said.

Hannah nodded. "You're right. Ficus it is."

"I'm glad we got that settled."

She was so lost in thought that his dry tone went right over Hannah's head. "So am I. It's one less thing to worry about. Oh, you'd never imagine what we found when we pulled up the linoleum in the dining room today."

"The bodies of everyone who died of ptomaine poisoning from eating Johnny's cooking?"

They were sitting on the overstuffed couch in front of the fire. Sometime during Hannah's lengthy discourse, Trace had put his arm along the back of the blue-and-red chintz cushions. Encouraged when Hannah didn't move away, he allowed his hand to slip down and rest on her shoulder. Just like high school, he thought. Trying to get up the nerve to neck with Mary Jane Miller in the back row

of New Chance's Penultimate Picture Palace, the town's
one movie theater.

"Oak plank flooring." She smiled up at him. "It must be
the original floor—it's all hand-fitted tongue and groove.
Isn't that marvelous?"

"Marvelous," he murmured distractedly. Her soft scent
was swirling around his head, making it difficult to concentrate.

"Oh, dear."

"Something wrong with the ficus after all?"

"No, I just realized that I've been talking nonstop about
myself and not letting you get a word in edgewise."

"That's okay. I'm perfectly content to just sit here and
smell your neck."

He felt her stiffen slightly. "Really, Trace . . ."

"Really." He nuzzled the soft skin above the neckline of
her crimson sweater. "You always smell like sunlit mead-
ows after a warm spring rain. Can I help it if it makes me
think about making love to you?"

"You shouldn't talk like that," she whispered.

"And you shouldn't smell so good." He skimmed his
fingertips down her neck. "Or feel so good." His lips followed the trail his fingers had left, warming her skin,
causing her to tremble. "Or taste so good."

"Trace." It was little more than a whisper, but easily
heard in the stillness of the room. A log shifted, sending
up a scattered flare of sparks that were reflected in the luminous gleam of her eyes.

He pushed aside the cowl neck of the sweater, permitting his roving lips access to the silky skin of her shoulder.
"Is that a complaint?" he murmured huskily. "Or an invitation?"

If she knew that, Hannah mused through the golden
mist that had begun to cloud her mind, she wouldn't be so

confused. Part of her wanted Trace Murphy, more than she could remember wanting anything in her life. Another part—the pragmatic side she'd been forced to develop over these past painful months—coaxed caution.

Trace could feel her building hunger. He could feel it in the way her body trembled under his increasingly intimate touch. He could feel it in the quickening of her pulse, he could see it in the way her eyes were turning to a dark and gleaming pewter as they gazed back into his. But he could feel her vacillating as well. Her hands were pressed against his chest, as if trying to decide whether to clutch at him, or push him away. Slowly, reluctantly, he solved the problem for her by backing away.

"You are so lovely," he said softly. He ran the back of his hand down the side of her face. "I can't remember ever seeing anyone with skin as fair as yours."

Hannah wanted to grab hold of his hand and press it to her lips. "It doesn't tan."

"Tans are highly overrated. They also give you wrinkles." A vision appeared in his mind: a vision of Hannah, cooking Sunday dinner for a passel of grandchildren, her face smooth and unlined and looking every bit as radiant as it did at this moment. "Did I thank you for dinner?"

"You did. Several times. Did I thank you for the wine?"

"Three times."

"I guess we've covered everything, then."

"I suppose so. Except for what you're doing next Thursday."

"Next Thursday?" she asked blankly.

"Thanksgiving."

Of course, she remembered now. That's why Scott had come home from school wearing that Pilgrim hat made out of construction paper.

"I suppose I'll fix a turkey and pie for Scott, then spend the rest of the day working."

"At the restaurant."

"Where else?"

Where else, indeed. Trace had heard the stories of Hannah's workaholic habits. Dan had told him that although all the men tried to insist she take a break from time to time, she steadfastly refused, leaving them feeling guilty when they left her alone, still slaving away, at the end of the day.

Trace took hold of her hand and turned it over. Her soft skin was marred by angry blisters at the base of each finger. A few of the blisters were hardening to calluses. "Look at what you're doing to yourself," he said.

"Those calluses are merely the sign of hard, honest work," she countered. "Do you have something against work, Sheriff?"

"Of course not. Do you have something against moderation?"

"There'll be time for moderation once the Red Rock reopens for business."

Trace wondered about that; from what he'd seen and heard about Hannah Greene, the lady was definitely driven. He understood ambition, could even respect it, but he couldn't shake the feeling that Hannah was carrying things too far.

"Look, I understand your desire to get the place open, but you can't keep working around the clock indefinitely."

"It's not indefinite. With any luck the restaurant will be open before Christmas. I'd already decided to run ads in the Sedona and Flagstaff papers, but Mitzi suggested that since people like to vacation in the mountains during the holidays, I should consider advertising in the Phoenix papers, as well. Of course the advertising rates are a lot higher in the city, but if I could pick up some repeat vacation business, the additional cost might be worth it. What do you think?"

"I think you're working too hard."

He hadn't bothered to censor the irritation in his voice and Hannah was amazed at how his disapproval had the power to hurt her. She had a sudden, almost reckless urge to tell him the truth. To tell him about David, about his death and everything that followed. But how could she explain that it was fear, not ambition that kept her going? Fear of failure. Fear of discovering that she was incapable of taking care of herself. Of Scott.

"Thank you for your concern, but I don't believe that's any of your business, Sheriff."

Her tone was cool and more than a little patronizing. Trace's anger flared, but he controlled it...until he looked down at her roughened palms and her ragged, torn fingernails. The soft shadows he'd witnessed under her eyes that first night had deepened, appearing like bruises against her creamy skin. Although he was admittedly no expert on female bodies, he'd have sworn she'd lost weight, too. Ambition was one thing. Blind ambition yet another.

"Now there's where you're wrong, sweetheart," he retorted. "Your son just happens to have made it my business."

"Scott?" She looked at him disbelievingly. "What does Scott have to do with this."

"How about the fact that he's forced to talk to a virtual stranger about his father because his mother's too damn immersed in her career to listen?"

The breath flew out of her lungs as if he'd hit her in the stomach with his fist. Every bit of color fled Hannah's face;

her eyes brimmed with sudden, hot tears she refused to allow herself to shed.

Trace damned his reckless words the moment he heard them escape his lips. His hands moved to her shoulders, and his eyes, as he looked down into her too-pale face, were filled with regret. "Hey, I'm sorry," he said. "That was a low blow. And entirely without foundation."

"No. You're right, Scott doesn't talk with me about David. I've tried, several times, but he always changes the subject."

She was tense. Too tense. His palms caressed her shoulders, seeking to soothe the cruelly twisted muscles. "He's afraid of hurting your feelings." Her obvious pain, shimmering in her moist gray eyes, tore at something deep inside Trace. "It seems he's got the mistaken impression that it's his job to protect you."

"The man of the house." Hannah gave a long, weary sigh. "I wasn't the one who put that idea into his head." It was important that he understand at least that much. "Really, I wasn't."

He pressed his lips against her temple. Her skin was cold and dry. "I know." Ambitious Hannah might be. Even driven. But she was not the type to play complex emotional games, especially with a child.

"The first time I heard him make that ridiculous statement was at the funeral, when he assured the Reverend Miller that we'd be okay. Seven years old, and he was suddenly the self-proclaimed man of the house. I couldn't believe my ears. If it wasn't so tragic, it might be funny."

"I think it's genetic," he said soothingly. "Woven into a male's DNA, carried over from when men left their caves each morning with their sturdy clubs over their shoulders and returned back to hearth and home each evening with a bunch of brontosaurus steaks."

"It's crazy."

"Probably. But I wouldn't worry too much about Scott, Hannah. He seems to be doing okay."

"It's been a—" Her breathing grew jerky, and she took a moment to compose herself. "—difficult time," she said finally.

"I can imagine."

"I've tried to give Scott the stability I knew he needed, but there was so much to do." She gave him a weary look. "So much to do."

Her hands were twisting agitatedly in her lap. Trace captured them in his. "You have to give yourself—and Scott—time, Hannah. Even Rome wasn't built in a day."

"I'm not worried about Rome—it's getting the Red Rock renovated in time for the holidays that concerns me."

"Dammit, this isn't a marathon. And you're not running against any clock."

It was so easy for him, Hannah mused. He was a man. A man accustomed not only to controlling his own life, but as sheriff, to holding power over the lives of so many others as well. How could he ever understand the doubts that hovered continuously over her head like a gray and threatening cloud?

"I have to have the Red Rock open by Christmas," she insisted once again.

Stubborn. The word didn't even begin to describe this woman. Trace told himself that the smart thing to do would be to get off this couch, march out the door to his Jeep and drive away, leaving the delectable, but frustratingly intransigent Hannah Greene to her unbridled Eastern ambition.

"So what, exactly, would happen if you didn't get the place open by Christmas? Would the world as we know it come to an end? Would thousands of vacationers starve without the chance to sample a piece of Hannah Greene's incomparable mincemeat pie? Would the entire economic foundation of the western world crumble down around our feet?"

"I'd run out of money, that's what would happen!" Irritation, fueled by her own fears that she wouldn't complete the restoration in time, caused Hannah's temper to flare. Jerking her hands away, she jumped to her feet.

Trace watched as she crossed the room to the window and stared out into the slanting silver rain. He'd suspected her funds were limited, but he hadn't realized that she was in danger of completely running out of money.

"I didn't know."

"Well, now you do." She leaned her forehead against the windowpane and closed her eyes. Moisture streamed down the outside of the window; the glass felt cool and soothing against her skin. "I'm sorry."

"If anyone needs to apologize, Hannah, it's me. I had no right to push."

"I shouldn't have flown off the handle like that." She let out an unsteady breath. "And I definitely shouldn't have taken my troubles out on you."

"That's what friends are for," he said simply.

She considered his words for a long time before turning back toward him. "Is that what we are?" she asked quietly. "Friends?"

In spite of the sudden seriousness of the conversation, Trace couldn't resist a slight smile. "You're an intelligent woman, Hannah. Surely it hasn't escaped your attention that I'd like to be a great deal more than a friend." He paused, watching the soft color drifting into her cheeks in confirmation of his words. "But if you're not ready, I'd settle for friends." For now, he tacked on silently.

"We don't even know each other."

"I think we're beginning to," he countered. "Besides, I know Scott, and there's a great deal of you in your son, Mrs. Greene."

For some reason she could not quite discern, Hannah appreciated the reference to her marriage. It made her feel as if Trace might understand her hesitation. Her confusion. She'd been married to David Greene for so many years that even though she knew it was silly, her instant, unexpected attraction to this man made her feel vaguely adulterous.

"Do you think so?" she asked softly.

"I know so. There's obviously a lot of your husband in Scott, too. From everything he's told me, it sounds as if David was a wonderful man." There, he'd done it. After thinking almost nonstop about his rival for two weeks, Trace had finally said the man's name out loud.

"He was."

"Scott worries that you still miss his father." Although he'd promised himself that he wouldn't pry, Trace couldn't quite keep the question from his voice.

Confused, and very tired from her hours of work at the Red Rock, Hannah dragged her hand through her hair. "I do still miss him," she admitted. "Oh, not as much as I used to. But there are times, when something good happens, like finding that floor today, when I instinctively turn around to share it with him."

"I can understand that." He'd been there himself, Trace thought, remembering all the times after Ellen's death that he'd found himself talking to her picture, sharing bits and pieces of his day with her.

"Or when I'm afraid," Hannah continued, "or late at night, when I'm alone in bed, and . . ." Her cheeks flamed as Hannah realized she was about to reveal her most intimate secret.

Trace flashed her a quirky grin. "I'm well acquainted with that one." Before he found himself volunteering to help her out on that score, Trace decided the time had come to turn the conversation back to something less personal.

"I'm afraid the job of sheriff doesn't pay all that much, at least probably not what you're used to, but I have managed to put some money away, Hannah. You're welcome to as much as you need."

There was no sign of guile in his emerald eyes. The offer was as open and honest as the man himself. All the more reason she could never accept it.

"Thank you, Trace, I appreciate your offer, really I do, but this is something I have to do myself."

Trace could understand pride, having a fair share of it himself. Accepting much-needed help was one thing, charity was quite another, and there was a razor-thin line between the two.

"I wasn't offering you charity."

"Weren't you?"

"No. It was more in the line of a loan. Or, if you'd rather, an investment."

He'd caught her unwilling interest with that one. "In the Red Rock?"

"No, in the lady running the Red Rock," he countered. "But I suppose that in the long run it works out the same."

Hannah caught her bottom lip between her teeth as she considered his offer. She couldn't deny that she was in desperate need of money. Despite the lowered price she'd paid for the Red Rock, everything was turning out to cost a great deal more than she'd planned. Even with all the free help she'd been getting, even with all the hours of work she'd put in herself, every time she turned around, it seemed as if another delivery man was standing there with his hand out.

"I'll think about it," she said finally.

It wasn't much, Trace decided, but it was a start. "You do that." He rose from the couch, reluctantly deciding that he'd made about as much progress as he could hope to this evening. Although he'd always considered himself a fairly easygoing individual, he was rapidly discovering an impatient streak he had been unaware of possessing.

"I'd better be going so Mildred MacGregor can get some sleep."

Hannah smiled as she walked with him to the door. "I really did have a lovely evening."

"We'll have to do it again sometime."

"I'd like that," she said, realizing she meant it. "Thank you for being so nice to Scott."

"I've already told you, Hannah, Scott's a super kid. It's easy to be nice to him. Damn."

She looked up at him curiously. "What's the matter?"

"I was supposed to tell you that Dan and Mitzi want you and Scott to have Thanksgiving dinner out at the ranch."

The idea was extremely tempting. "I'm sorry, but I—"

"Have to work."

She didn't hesitate. "Yes."

His gaze moved over her face, taking in the calm, unwavering determination in her eyes, the taut, thin line of her unpainted lips. He wanted Hannah, more than he could ever remember wanting a woman, and he felt certain that were it not for that damned Red Rock Café, he and the lovely widow would not be wasting time talking about linoleum and trees and the difference between oil- and water-based paints. The solution to his dilemma was readily apparent: if he wanted to make love to Hannah, he'd simply have to help her get the place open. As soon as possible.

Hannah watched Trace warily; his slight sigh sounded more thoughtful than annoyed. "If I promise that the Red Rock will be open by Christmas, will you take off just one day for some much needed R and R?"

"How can you guarantee something like that?"

"Believe me, Hannah, I never promise anything I can't deliver."

The funny thing, Hannah thought, was that she believed him. Almost. "I don't know," she murmured, tempted by the idea of a day away from the restaurant. A day where she could relax and enjoy herself for a change.

"Scott would enjoy the day at the ranch a lot more than he would hanging around the restaurant while you sand floors," he coaxed. "Dad's already promised to teach him how to ride."

"It's unfair to use my own son against me."

His grin was quick, devilish and too, too appealing. "Is it working?"

Hannah's frustrated sigh ruffled her dark bangs. "Of course it's working." She frowned at him. "If I take the day off and the Red Rock doesn't open for Christmas—"

He held up a hand. "It'll open on time. Trust me."

Hannah decided that she did. "Do you always get exactly what you want?"

Trace thought of Ellen, of the giddy, love-filled plans they'd made, of the children dreamed about but never born. "No. Not always."

The fleeting sadness in his eyes came and went so quickly that had Hannah not been watching him so closely, she might have thought she imagined it. Although she wondered at the cause, she decided that there

had been more than enough personal revelations for one
evening and didn't pursue it.

"Just most of the time," she suggested quietly.

"Most of the time," Trace agreed. He reached for her
hair; the sleek dark strands felt like silk as they flowed
through his fingers. "Speaking of wants, do you have any
idea how much I want to kiss you? It's almost all I've been
able to think about for days."

He was close. Close enough for Hannah to read his intent in his warming gaze. She should resist, she told herself. Now, quickly, while she was capable of coherent
thought. When his arm snaked around her waist, she knew
a prudent woman would back away. But she remained
where she was, entranced by the temptation gleaming in
his eyes. When he lowered his head, Hannah rose onto her
toes to meet his lips with her own.

A clap of thunder reverberated in her head, lightning
rocketed up her spine, heat infused her bloodstream. Desire, ripe and unrestrained enveloped her, creating a hunger she'd never known, needs she'd never imagined. She
clutched at him, her own avid lips turning greedy—responding, demanding, thrilling.

Excitement swirled in the hot, steamy air surrounding
them, raw passion poured from one into the other. Her soft
sighs and moans, as she arched against him, were a sensual symphony to his ears, and her hands, as they
skimmed up and down his back like quicksilver, caused
his skin to grow hot and sensitized. Delving under the
scarlet sweater, Trace felt her heart pounding against his
palm. She was small and firm, her skin satin-soft and ra-
diantly warm. And he wanted her with a desperate need
that bordered on insanity.

He dragged his mouth away from hers, burying his lips
in the perfumed silk of her hair. "Let's move this into your

bedroom." He drew her closer, pressing her against the rock-hard strength of his arousal. "Where we can lock the door and see how long it takes to drive each other crazy."

Excitement thrummed through her body; anticipation shimmered across her skin. Fascinated, and more than a little tempted to test this phenomenon further, Hannah closed her eyes, reveling in the way his thumb and finger were creating havoc on the already taut peak of her breast.

"I can't think."

"Then don't." He crushed his lips to hers again, satisfied when he felt her yielding. "Just feel," he crooned as his hand moved between them down her body to the waistband of her jeans. "Feel how good we'd be together."

The unmistakable sound of the snap, followed by the slow, steady lowering of the metal zipper was loud in the stillness of the night. "Trace . . ."

"You are so soft," he murmured huskily, refusing to hear her ragged complaint. "So lovely."

Her mind was clouded by a red, glowing mist, her body hummed with a thousand tiny pulses, but even as she felt herself succumbing to the skill of those clever, wicked hands and the dark, mysterious taste of his mouth, Hannah struggled for a last grasp at sanity.

"Trace," she said with a gasp as his fingers skimmed tantalizingly along the waistband of her cotton bikini panties. "I can't do this."

He drew her closer when she would have moved away. "You can't deny that you want me as much as I want you."

"No." She put both her hands on his shoulders and pushed. "No, I can't. But just because I want to make love with you doesn't mean that I'm going to do it."

"Why not?"

Hannah backed away, her numb fingers fumbling embarrassingly with the zipper of her jeans. Her breath was coming hard and fast, like a runner who'd just finished an Olympic marathon. "Because wanting's not enough."

Damn. Even as he wanted to drag her into her bedroom and prove to her that she was making the mistake of her life by sending him away tonight, Trace knew that she was right. With some women—free-spirited women accustomed to following their feelings—desire would be more than enough. With Hannah, things would always be more serious. More complicated. It was just as well, Trace decided with a fatalism that had served him well for the past thirty-five years. Experience had taught him that things that came too easily were often not worth having at all.

Patience, he warned himself. Some things—some women—were worth waiting for. "I'm a reasonably patient man, Hannah. I'm willing to wait."

"You'll have a very long wait."

Her eyes were wide gray pools of need; her cheeks were flushed a bright pink that brought to mind roses blooming in the snow. Trace couldn't remember ever seeing anything so lovely. Couldn't remember wanting anyone quite as much as he wanted Hannah at this moment.

"Perhaps." He ran a slow, teasing fingertip over her swollen mouth. "And then again, perhaps not." He opened the door, letting in a gust of brisk November air.

And then he disappeared into the night, leaving Hannah shaken and wanting.

6

THINGS WERE BEGINNING to take shape. The peeling olive-drab paint had been replaced by a warm Navaho-white enamel, which in turn made the polished copper hood seem to gleam even more brightly. Pouring herself a cup of coffee from the carafe of the new drip coffee maker—one glance at Johnny's oil-encrusted stainless-steel vat had been more than enough to make her throw it away—Hannah leaned back against the counter to savor her feeling of satisfaction. For the first time since she'd begun the Herculean task of renovating the Red Rock Café, she could actually envision the restaurant opening on time.

"Looking good." A familiar deep voice broke into her reverie.

Her fingers tightened on the Styrofoam coffee cup as she slowly turned around. Trace was standing in the doorway, looking better than any man had a right to look.

"It is, isn't it? I had a terrible time deciding what color to paint the walls—you've no idea how many shades of white there are—but I think it turned out perfectly. It's bright, but it has a warm undertone that complements the copper, don't you think?"

This time the red sweatshirt, with a silk-screened picture of a fat striped cat, advertised the wonders of the Metropolitan Museum of Art, and her jeans were worn white at the stress points. In what Trace took to be a rare display of feminine vanity, a pair of milky pearls that had the same soft glow as her skin gleamed at her ears. He reminded himself that patience was reputed to be a virtue.

"It's great. But I wasn't talking about the paint, Hannah. I was talking about the painter."

She shook her head, even as her lips curved into a reluctant smile. "Don't you ever give up?"

"Not when it's something I want badly enough. And I believe we've already determined that I want you, Hannah."

"Really, Trace . . ."

"I see you got rid of the steer," he said, changing the subject before she could continue her complaint.

"The steer? Oh, you mean that big brown cow that was up on the roof. Yes, Cal Potter took it down for me this morning."

"That old steer's been a fixture on the Red Rock since before I was born," Trace remarked. "It'll seem kind of strange, having it gone."

"It isn't exactly gone."

"Really? What did you do with it?"

"Promise not to tell Scott?"

Trace held up his right hand as if making a pledge. "Promise. What's the matter, Hannah, are you afraid he'll ride his bike out to the dump, retrieve it and bring it back?"

"It's not at the dump."

"You put it out in your garden to use as a gigantic scarecrow," he guessed.

"Close. I had Cal put the cow—"

"Steer," Trace corrected.

Hannah shot him a frustrated look. "Cow, steer, what's the difference?"

"Let's just say that a steer is a bull who's lost his motivation for getting up in the morning. Actually, if you want to get technical, the poor guy can't get up at all."

As his green eyes danced, Hannah felt color flood her cheeks. "Oh. Well, anyway, I scrubbed it with hot soapy water and disinfectant and had Cal take it over to the house and put it in Scott's room for a surprise."

She'd been afraid Trace would laugh at her. Instead, his expression was approving. "That's great, Hannah. Scott's wild about that steer. He was really feeling bad when he thought you were going to get rid of it."

"I know. That's why I decided to do it. That and the desire to come up with something that could compete with those bank robber's fingerprints you gave him last night."

He lifted a brow. "I hadn't realized we were in competition."

"Aren't we?"

He shrugged. "Perhaps about some things, like how soon I can get you into my bed and how long you can resist. But not about Scott, Hannah. Believe me, we both have your son's best interests at heart."

No. Things were becoming too complicated too quickly. Desire was one thing. Hannah could deal with that. Well, perhaps not exactly deal with it, she considered, thinking how close she'd come to giving in last night. But she could accept it. However, allowing Trace to become close to Scott was entering into something far more serious than a fleeting sexual encounter. Scott had already been hurt enough; Hannah wasn't about to risk his happiness for a few moments of her own pleasure.

"You haven't told me what you're doing here, Sheriff."

Her tone was cool. Remote. Resisting the urge to grab her by the shoulders and shake some sense into her, Trace crossed the room and poured himself a cup of coffee.

"This is good," he said, looking down into his cup with surprise. "What did you do with Johnny's battery-acid maker?"

"If you're talking about that horrid stainless-steel vat, I threw it out. And if your sole reason for dropping by was to have a cup of coffee, now that you've had it, I'm sure you'll want to be on your way."

Leaning against the counter, appearing to be in no hurry to leave, he sipped appreciatively at the coffee. "The woman makes terrific cheeseburgers and great coffee," he said reflectively. "Not to mention being beautiful and a dynamite kisser. The man who wins your heart and hand, Mrs. Greene, is going to be one helluva lucky guy."

"Neither my heart nor my hand happen to be up for grabs," she said evenly. "Now, if you don't mind, I have a great deal of work to do." She turned away, picked up her brush and began covering yet another wall with paint.

She'd coated herself in enough ice to cover Jupiter, Trace thought, but he wasn't daunted. He'd already discovered the volcano lurking beneath that frosty exterior. "I know you do. That's why I'm here."

She glanced suspiciously over her shoulder. He was dressed in a khaki-colored uniform whose sharp creases could have cut diamonds. The fawn Stetson was on his head, his boots were polished to a gleaming shine and a service revolver rested in a leather holster against his hip. He certainly didn't look like a man prepared to do manual labor.

"You're here to paint walls?" she asked incredulously.

"Not exactly."

"I didn't think so."

"Hey, you're lucky I'm not volunteering—I'm a terrible painter. But I have brought you a restaurant-warming gift."

"An automatic paint sprayer?"

"Better."

Frustrated, Hannah turned around, put down her brush, and crossed her arms over her chest. "Are you going to let me in on exactly what this gift is or is it a secret?"

The grin broadened. "A fireplace."

Hannah stared at him. "A what?"

"A fireplace. Didn't you tell me last night that you wanted a beehive fireplace in the dining room?"

"I hadn't realized you were listening to anything I said last night."

Trace's smile didn't fade in wattage, but a gentle censure appeared in his eyes. "Just because I want to make love to you doesn't mean I wasn't listening, Hannah. I heard everything you said."

The intimate affection in his gaze tugged at something deep inside her. "Then you should recall that I'd decided I couldn't afford to put one in."

"Now that you mention it, that statement does seem to ring a bell."

"And I also told you that I didn't want to borrow any of your money."

"I remember. Although you promised to consider taking on a partner."

"I only promised to think about it," she reminded him. "And, if you want to know the truth—"

He held up his hand, forestalling what he perceived to be her imminent refusal. "The fireplace isn't going to cost a cent, Hannah. Hank Young has already volunteered to donate the supplies. And I've got one of the best stonemasons in the county sitting outside in my truck right now."

"Mr. Young has already donated the roofing material and been kind enough to give me a contractor's discount on the paint and other supplies. Why would he want to give me anything else?"

"Simple. He's getting hungry and figures that anything he can do to get the Red Rock reopened in a hurry will be worth the price."

"I don't understand."

"Hank's a bachelor. He's getting sick and tired of eating out of cans. Besides, it just so happens that his brother-in-law, Willard, ordered too many bricks from the supplier three months ago, and it's getting expensive to keep carrying them on the books."

"Why do I have the feeling he didn't make this generous decision all on his own?" she inquired suspiciously.

Trace shrugged. "Beats me. So, how about it, Hannah, do I bring the stuff in, or not?"

"Even if you're telling the truth about the material, I'm not certain I can accept."

"Why not?"

"Because it's a time-consuming, difficult job and anyone who actually knows how to build a fireplace is a skilled craftsman who deserves to be paid for his labor. And I really don't think I can afford it."

"I've got that all taken care of."

"I'm almost afraid to ask."

"It's simple. Building your fireplace is a condition of Jake's parole."

"Parole?" Hannah was beginning to get a headache. She rubbed her fingertips against her throbbing temples. "Your bricklayer is a prisoner?"

"In a manner of speaking. It's sort of complicated to explain."

The pounding in her head increased. "Why don't you try?" she suggested with a trace of irritation she didn't bother to hide.

Trace took his time answering. Hannah watched as he began idly drawing circles in the sawdust on the counter with his fingertip. The small, concentric lines reminded her of the way those wide dark hands had moved over her body last night, causing a glimmer of heat to race up her spine then down again. It wasn't wise being alone with a man who could make her feel that way, Hannah realized. Not wise at all.

"Jake's had a run of bad luck, lately," Trace said finally. As he switched to squares, the brim of his hat shielded his eyes from her view. "Drought two years in a row cost him most of his cash crop, then his cattle got anthrax. Anthrax is a severe bacterial disease," he explained at her questioning look. "It's highly contagious to both man and animal. Animals contract it by eating contaminated food. People usually contract it by eating contaminated meat."

"So when cattle contract it, they have to be destroyed," she guessed correctly.

He lifted his head to meet her knowing gaze. "He lost his entire herd."

"That's terrible. Isn't there any way to prevent it?"

"There are vaccinations, and Jake had all his cattle inoculated, but for some reason the stuff didn't take. The state health department's looking into that particular batch of vaccine, but even if they find it's defective, it isn't going to get Jake his herd back."

"He could always sue the manufacturer."

"If it turns out to be a bad vaccine, he'll probably do exactly that. He's also considering a suit against the manufacturer of the feed. But in the meantime, he's flat out of money and about to be run off his land."

"Oh no." Personal economic disaster was something Hannah could empathize with.

"As rotten as Jake's luck has been, I think he could live with that. After all, it's part of the gamble of living off the land. His granddaddy knew that ranching was a gamble, his daddy knew it, and Jake knew it. The problem is, he's convinced that the government's taking his land illegally."

"Surely you don't believe that."

"I don't think anyone would do such a thing intentionally," Trace agreed thoughtfully. "But Jake insists he made all his payments on time and I've never known him to lie." He flashed her a quick grin. "Unless it's about the size of the fish that got away, or the ten-point buck he almost shot or that redheaded waitress down in Cortez Junction who's supposedly been lusting after his body for the past ten years."

"It sounds as if you know this Jake well."

"His land borders on Dad's, and he's always been like an uncle to me. A favorite uncle." Trace decided that since Hannah had displayed a discouraging lack of interest in his personal life, there was no reason to add the fact that he'd been married to Jake's daughter.

"And now you're forced to arrest him."

His wide shoulders in the crisp khaki uniform lifted in a broad shrug. "He's not really that bad, Hannah. The poor guy just gets frustrated, has too much to drink, then gets rowdy. I want to go into Phoenix today and see if I can track down someone willing to go searching for the payments he swears he's made, and the truth is, I'm asking you to baby-sit him while I'm gone. If he's busy building your fireplace, he won't be getting into trouble."

"You're going to take on the federal government, all by yourself, even knowing it's a maze of red tape." For some reason, Hannah wasn't as surprised as she once might have been.

"Red tape Jake's gotten himself tangled up in," Trace said. "Somebody's got to help, and it may as well be me. After all, it is—"

"Part of the job," she finished for him, knowing that was far from the case.

"Something like that," Trace agreed with a faint smile. "I promise I wouldn't bring him down here if I thought there was any danger to you. Or to Scott." He lifted his gaze to hers. "Whatever doubts you may have about me personally, Hannah, you have to believe this."

Hannah had no doubt he was telling the truth. "You're a good friend," she said quietly.

Amusement. Desire. Affection. All were present in his smiling eyes. "That's what I've been trying to tell you."

He crossed the kitchen until he was standing directly in front of her. Unexpectedly, he ran his knuckles down her cheek in a way that was as gentle as it was unmistakably possessive.

"You've got paint on your face."

"That's no big surprise. My claim to fame is that I'm fast. I never claimed to be neat."

"Good thing. You've also got a white nose."

Tilting her head, Hannah frowned up at him even as her lips were threatening to break into a smile. "Are you going to spend all morning criticizing my painting skills, or are you going to introduce me to my fireplace builder?"

"In a minute." He picked up a turpentine-damp rag from the counter and rubbed at the white spot on her cheek. "That's better." Trace rubbed his chin as he studied her thoughtfully. "Perhaps we should leave the nose as it is— it's actually kind of cute. It makes you look more accessible."

Tossing the rag back onto the counter, he curved his fingers around the back of her neck. "Do you know what I did after leaving your house last night?"

"What?"

"I went home and spent several long and frustrating hours fantasizing about making love to you."

"Really, Trace . . ."

The slight tightening of his fingers on her nape was the only sign he'd heard her. "I imagined pulling you down onto that bright and homey rag rug in front of the fireplace and undressing you, taking off your clothing piece by piece, until your skin was gleaming in the flickering glow of the firelight."

The evocative vision was too close to some of the fantasies she'd been having lately. "Please," she whispered, "you shouldn't . . ."

He was only touching her neck, but his gaze had the physical impact of a caress as it moved down her body, and Hannah felt herself responding to his arousing words. Her blood began to heat, then a throbbing began—in her throat, in her chest, then lower—until it was all she could do not to fling her arms around him and drag him down to the sawdust-covered floor.

"And then," his deep, hypnotizing voice continued, "after I'd caressed every inch of that creamy flesh, I'd enter you slowly, giving you time to adjust to my incredible—"

Despite the fact he was driving her crazy, Hannah couldn't resist a half smile. "Incredible?"

"Just wait," he promised easily, bending his head to brush his lips briefly, without pressure or force, against hers. "And then we'd race the wind, Hannah. You and I. Together. Higher and higher, and faster and faster. And when we reached the edge of the sky and beyond, you'd realize that our lovemaking was every bit as perfect as it was inevitable."

"Well," Hannah said with a ragged breath, "no one could ever accuse you of having an underactive imagination, Trace Murphy. Or a less than robust ego."

"Just calling them like I see them," he said. "Besides, as I was saying, that's how I imagined making love to you last night. Seeing you in the bright light of day, with paint on your nose, has altered things."

"Changed your mind?"

Why, oh why, did she find that idea vastly disappointing? She had no intention of becoming involved with Trace. None at all. And anyone foolish enough to believe that would be a prime candidate for ocean-front property in New Chance, she admitted reluctantly.

"Oh, not about the act, just the location." His smile was quick, sexy and dangerous. "I don't know if it's the paint, or the way those jeans fit your tight little behind, but I have a sudden urge to spend the day tumbling you in my father's hayloft."

He nibbled on her neck, inhaling her fresh, wildflower scent. "How about it, Hannah, my sweet," he murmured enticingly. "Have you ever made love in a bed of hay?"

Even as she sought to ignore the havoc his teeth were creating, Hannah's rebellious mind conjured up the pungent scent of straw, warmed by a slanting buttery sunbeam. Trace's skin, where the sun touched it, would be dark, contrasting vividly with the bright yellow straw, and his body, as it pressed against hers, would be hot and hard and . . .

No. It was happening all over again. Ducking out of his light embrace, Hannah grabbed up the wet rag and began scrubbing furiously at her nose. "You have to stop talking like this," she hissed. "Someone might hear you."

If Trace was annoyed by her refusal to give in, his easy-going expression failed to reveal it. "Cal and Fred are outside tarring the roof, Dad drove out to the ranch to get some linseed oil for these cabinets and Jake's still sitting out in the truck, waiting for the okay to come in."

He looked at her flushed skin, her soft pink mouth and wondered if the lovely Widow Greene had the slightest idea what she did to him. One glance from those wide gray eyes, a single touch from those pale, slender hands, and he'd be undone.

"You don't have to worry, Hannah," he said quietly. "We're all alone."

That knowledge did nothing to instill calm. Hannah glanced pointedly down at her watch. The face was spattered with pinpoint drops of white paint, but she could still read the Roman numerals. "If you're planning to get any work done in Phoenix, I'd suggest you leave now. Government employees have a habit of closing up shop and going home earlier than the rest of us."

Unfortunately, as much as he wanted her, even now, this was neither the time or the place. There'd be another day, Trace reminded himself reluctantly. Another time.

"In a minute." He plucked the rag from her trembling hands and disposed of the remainder of the white paint on her face with a few deft strokes. Then he kissed her, a long and lingering kiss that threatened to take her breath away.

It wasn't supposed to be like this, Trace thought as he felt the floor begin slipping away from under him. He was the pursuer, Hannah was the prey. It was only right that she'd tremble when he touched her, flame when his lips warmed her flesh. From that first startled moment of recognition, Trace had enjoyed knowing that he could disconcert the lovely young widow. He'd also enjoyed the sexual tension that had been humming between them from the beginning.

Even though that first kiss had admittedly shaken him to the core, Trace had been able to explain away his reaction as surprise at discovering such passion inside an outwardly cool woman. Comfortable with that conclusion, he'd not dwelled on it any longer. But now, as Hannah's lips moved avidly, greedily on his and her hands gripped his arms, as if she, too, could feel the earth tilting on its axis, Trace realized that he was rapidly losing the battle.

He was being absorbed by her, drowning in the warmth of her soft and feminine body as she arched upward, fitting herself unerringly to his stirring hardness. He'd wanted her because she was an attractive, intelligent woman who roused something inside him. Trace had never claimed to live a celibate life and wasn't about to apologize for wanting to bed Hannah.

But what had begun as mere desire was rapidly turning into something that smacked of obsession. The almost desperate, uncontrollable need for her grated against his pride. A less self-assured man would have been infuriated or frightened by his lack of self-control; Trace opted merely to leave while he still maintained some vestige of sanity. He'd think about this during the long, solitary drive to Phoenix.

"I'll go get Jake," he suggested raggedly, once they'd come up for air.

Hannah's head was still spinning and she was swaying on her feet. It was all she could do to nod her consent. Trace had no sooner left the kitchen than she sank down onto a nearby stool and buried her face in her hands.

To HIS CREDIT, Jake Brennan did not look like a criminal. He was neatly dressed in a red plaid shirt and jeans; his scuffed brown boots had wedge heels that, along with his leather-dark skin, revealed a lifetime spent in the saddle. To Hannah's vast relief, he didn't behave like a criminal, either, but greeted her politely when Trace introduced them, exchanged greetings with the other men and went straight to work. Hannah returned to her painting.

By lunchtime, she had three of the four walls finished and was ready for a break. Taking a brown paper bag out of the refrigerator, she entered the dining room to find Jake still hard at work.

"Where are the others?" she asked, glancing around. Cal, Fred and Dan were nowhere to be seen.

"They went to pick up some supplies in Cottonwood. Said they'd get lunch there," he replied without turning around.

"Oh. What about you?"

"What about me?"

"Would you like some lunch?"

"Thanks, but I'd just as soon keep working, if it's all the same to you, ma'am."

"Surely you're hungry," Hannah coaxed.

Jake's only response, as he cut a brick in half, was a nonchalant shrug.

Well, at least she didn't have to worry about the man talking her to death. Hannah decided to try again. "I got a little carried away this morning," she said with a smile in her voice. "I'll never be able to eat all this by myself." Although she was loathe to admit it, the reason for all the extra food today was in case Trace had happened to drop by for lunch.

Nothing. Jake continued measuring and cutting.

"It's meat loaf," she offered.

Jake slowly put the saw down and turned around. "With ketchup?" he asked suspiciously.

"Tons."

"And onions?"

"Ever hear of a meat loaf without onions?" Hannah countered.

"I like mustard in it, too," he said, testing her further.

"Got it."

"The yellow kind, or that fancy European stuff they advertise on those television commercials?"

Strike one. "I'm afraid it's brown," she admitted reluctantly.

"Figures," Jake humphed. "I'm partial to the yellow kind, myself."

"I see." So was Scott, but Hannah didn't think it prudent to accuse the man of having the palate of an eight-year-old.

"No offense meant to your cooking, ma'am, but the yellow kind is spicier," Jake pointed out.

"No offense taken, Mr. Brennan," Hannah assured him. "However, this mustard has horseradish mixed into it."

He arched a wiry brown brow. "Horseradish?"

"That's right."

Hannah waited as Jake seemed to be thinking the matter over. "I guess horseradish might give it the right amount of kick," he allowed finally.

Hannah repressed her smile. "I've always thought so."

He rubbed his unshaven chin as his eyes drifted to the brown paper bag she was still holding in her hand. "I suppose I could give it a try. Seein' as how Trace didn't see fit to feed me a decent breakfast. Never have figured out how a grown man can eat all that sugarcoated cereal first thing in the morning," he complained. "Not to mention how the stuff turns the milk different colors." He fixed her with a direct gaze. "You ever try eating blue milk with a hangover?"

"No, I'm afraid that's one thing I've never experienced," Hannah murmured.

"Those Murphys always have been crazy. And Trace is the worst of the lot, 'cepting mebbe old Jedidiah."

"Jedidiah?"

"Trace's great-great-granddaddy. He founded New Chance."

"Did you spend the night with Trace?" she asked conversationally as she took out a foil-wrapped sandwich and handed it to him.

"In a way." He eyed her curiously. "Didn't Trace tell you? I spent last night in jail."

"Oh." Hannah was momentarily nonplussed. "I didn't know. I mean I did know that you've had a few unfortunate brushes with the law, but I hadn't realized that—"

"Trace arrested me for being drunk and disorderly outside Mel Skinner's house around about one o'clock this morning," Jake said matter-of-factly.

"Were you?" Hannah couldn't resist asking.

Again that uncaring shrug. "Sure. But I didn't have any choice. If the bastard would've let me in, I'd have been drunk and disorderly *inside* his house. That way I wouldn't have disrupted the neighborhood." He unwrapped the sandwich, wadded the tin foil into a ball and tossed it into a nearby cardboard box.

"Just Mr. Skinner's sleep."

"Hell—sorry about the language, ma'am—but Mel Skinner is nothing but a double-faced, two-tongued lying polecat. He deserves a helluva lot more than having his sleep disrupted. The fiend stole my money. Now he's tryin' to steal my land. My grandpappy's land." He took a forceful bite of the thick sandwich. "Well, I'm not about to let that happen," he mumbled around the slab of spiced meat loaf.

It was more than an idle threat made by a man with a hangover, Hannah knew. Viewing the icy determination in Jake Brennan's blue eyes, she found herself hoping that Trace would be able to solve Jake's problem with the government while in Phoenix this afternoon. Because, if not, he might just find himself having to arrest his friend for something a great deal more serious than being drunk and disorderly.

"This is real good," Jake said, breaking the silence that had settled around them.

Now that she'd witnessed the simmering anger inside Jake Brennan, Hannah no longer felt as comfortable around the man as she had earlier. "You sound surprised."

"I kinda figured you'd be one of those fancy Eastern cooks who liked to whip up things with fancy names nobody can ever pronounce. Stuff made outta eel gizzards, or brains, or some such thing."

"Eel gizzards?"

He nodded as he chewed. "Yeah, you know, all that highbrow stuff. Like raw fish."

"Sushi." She handed him a small Tupperware bowl of potato salad.

"That's it," he said around a mouthful of salad. "I used to have this lady friend. Taught English up at NAU—Northern Arizona University," he elaborated at her questioning glance. "Anyway, Kate came from back East, like you, and she was plumb crazy about the stuff. Acted kinda like a horse on locoweed, if you know what I mean."

"I believe I do," Hannah murmured. "And although I do like sushi myself, I've no plans to serve it in the Red Rock."

"Good idea," he agreed, looking over the food she'd spread out onto a two-by-four. "Wouldn't think you'd have too many customers if you did. Are you gonna eat that piece of pie?"

"It's yours," Hannah offered, handing over the piece of pecan pie she'd never had any intention of eating.

"This is damned good," Jake said, looking at her admiringly. "You're gonna do real well in New Chance, Miz Greene."

"I fervently hope so, Mr. Brennan," Hannah said.

He took another bite and rolled his eyes. "Real well," he repeated. "Folks around here like good basic food. Not like that raw fish stuff." His blue eyes danced with the first humor she'd seen him display. "Course we've had sushi around these parts for a real long time," he revealed. "Probably far back as the days New Chance was founded."

"Really?"

"Sure. But we've always called it bait."

When Hannah laughed, as she was supposed to, Jake grinned. The uncomfortable moment had passed.

7

"ARE YOU AND ME gonna have Thanksgiving alone again this year?" Scott asked as he set the kitchen table for dinner.

He'd dragged the cow—steer, Hannah corrected—from his room, unwilling to let it out of his sight. She knew it was silly, but she found herself hating the way it seemed to be staring at her through its dark brown glass eyes.

"You and I," she corrected.

"Are you and *I* gonna have Thanksgiving alone again this year?"

She stopped in the middle of mixing waffle batter. Cheeseburgers, pizza, waffles—for a restaurant owner, she certainly wasn't very innovative when it came to her home cooking, she considered. Then she decided she was lucky that Scott, like all eight year olds, much preferred chili to calamari, tuna to truffles.

"What's the matter, don't you like the company?"

"It's not that." He began twisting the paper napkin to shreds. "It's just that sometimes it's kind of nice to do something different."

"Such as having Thanksgiving dinner with Trace over at his father's house?"

He lifted slender shoulders in an exaggerated shrug. "I guess we could do that. If you wanted to."

"How about you? What do you want to do?"

He turned to her, his expression as earnest as Hannah had ever seen it. "Trace says I could ride one of his dad's horses, Mom. A real horse," he stressed. "Not like that stupid pony Bobby Erickson had for his birthday party last year."

Hannah poured the batter onto the preheated waffle iron and closed the lid. "Well, goodness," she murmured, "imagine that. A real horse."

"Well?"

The pieces of napkin scattered over the floor looked like pieces of Hansel and Gretel's trail out of the forest. Hannah handed him another. "I don't know, Scott," she said truthfully. "It's not as simple as it sounds."

Scott took a deep breath and blurted, "Is it because you don't like Trace?"

She would have had to have been deaf and blind not to hear the distress in her son's voice, see the anxiety written in bold script across his young face. "I like Trace," she hedged.

"He sure likes you," Scott revealed, placing the napkins beside the plates. The stainless steel cutlery—Hannah had sold her wedding silver—followed.

"Oh?" Disturbed that Trace was talking with Scott about her, perhaps even pumping him for information about her, Hannah vowed to speak to him first thing tomorrow morning.

"Yeah. Whenever I complain about having to do my homework, or going to bed before Miami Vice, or eating my vegetables, Trace tells me that I'm real lucky to have you for my mom."

"Really," she murmured.

"Yeah. But I already knew that. Could we, Mom? Please? I'll go to bed an hour early for a month."

"You don't have to do that."

"Then I promise never to call Mrs. MacGregor a snoopy old walrus again."

"Scott," she said, truly aghast, "surely you don't—"

"Gee, I don't call her that to her face. Just when I'm joking around with the guys." He took the milk carton from the refrigerator and filled his glass. "Want some?"

"Thank you, I think I would. And from now on, I don't want you insulting Mrs. MacGregor. Even to the guys."

"She does have a big old mustache, just like a walrus," Scott pointed out.

"Mrs. MacGregor's mustache is none of your concern, young man."

"And she's always snooping on everybody. Every night she asks me about back in Connecticut, and did you have any boyfriends after Dad died, and how often Trace visits us. It gets so bad I have to go into my room and do my homework, instead of watching TV."

Hannah wasn't surprised. Irritated, perhaps. But not surprised. "Well, a little extra studying certainly won't kill you," she said. "But I'll have a talk with Mrs. MacGregor and ask that she not discuss our personal life with you."

"Okay, but I bet it won't do any good. Warren says that back when New Chance had party lines, you could always hear her breathing on the line. I think she's nosy, Mom."

Hannah smiled at that. Reaching out, she ruffled her son's dark hair. "I think you're probably right, kiddo."

"So," Scott said, once they'd finished their light supper, "can we go over to the ranch for Thanksgiving?"

The thought of preparing an elaborate Thanksgiving dinner while she was working so hard at the Red Rock was less than appealing. When Hannah found herself tempted, she tried telling herself it was only to get out of all that cooking.

"I'll think about it."

"Gee, thanks, Mom." Scott threw his arms around her waist. "I knew you'd say yes."

"I said I'll *think* about it," Hannah reminded him.

"I know. But that's always what you say when you're going to give in."

"Is it?"

"Yep."

"Every time?"

He nodded. "Every time."

"Hmm," Hannah mused. "Perhaps to keep from being too predictable, I should say no. Just on general principle."

"Mom!"

She grinned. "I'll think about it."

Scott's young face relaxed into a broad grin of his own. "Thanks, Mom. You're the greatest."

NO ONE COULD HAVE BEEN more surprised than Hannah when Trace suddenly, without warning, changed tactics. The evening after his trip to Phoenix, he showed up at the Red Rock, declaring his intention to work. Although in the beginning, Hannah was afraid that his unexpected maneuver was merely another attempt to seduce her, her fears were quickly put to rest. Acting as if the sensual moments, the heated kisses had never occurred, he began treating her merely as a friend, rather than a potential lover.

Giving in to Scott's continual lobbying, Hannah spent Thanksgiving out at the ranch with Dan, Mitzi and Trace. Although Dan assured her that his housekeeper was quite capable of preparing dinner by herself, Hannah contributed a pumpkin cheesecake, which proved quite popular. The food was superb, the company more than congenial, the mood relaxed. It was, all in all, a very pleasant day.

After dinner Trace invited Hannah and Scott to go horseback riding, but too relaxed after the enormous meal to move, Hannah demurred. Scott, whom Dan had laughingly accused of having a hollow leg from the amount of turkey and stuffing he'd made disappear, proved more than eager, and Hannah knew she'd be hearing about this day for weeks to come.

The romance between Dan and Mitzi appeared to be in full bloom; they were constantly exchanging warm, intimate looks when they thought no one was looking. And once, when Hannah had taken a stack of dirty dishes into the kitchen, she inadvertently caught the pair in a remarkably steamy kiss.

Despite her happiness for the romantic couple, Hannah couldn't resist being a bit envious. And although she told herself that she should be grateful Trace had abandoned his sensual campaign, she found herself missing the way he had, for a short time, made her feel like a very desirable woman.

Over the next ten nights Trace proved himself a willing, albeit less than skilled manual laborer as he threw himself into his work with an enthusiasm that reminded her of Scott entering into a new project. He hadn't lied about his painting skills; they were, if anything, weaker than her own.

She set him to countersinking the nails on the shelves Cal Potter had built, but when he hit his thumb twice and scarred the dark oak with the head of the hammer on more than one occasion, Hannah sought to find something else to keep him occupied. When she suggested he help his father install the stained-glass window in the front door, Dan instantly threatened to quit if Trace got anywhere near his pet project.

Unfortunately, as bad as Trace's painting and carpentry skills were, he proved to be an impossible bricklayer. Ten minutes after he'd begun working as Jake's apprentice, the older man had threatened to quit if Hannah couldn't find something else for, in Jake's vernacular, "that ten-thumbed jackass" to do.

"The sink's been leaking in the men's rest room," she said thoughtfully as Trace stood cheerfully by, waiting for new orders. "How are you with plumbing?"

He shrugged. "I'll never know until I try."

His offhand answer didn't exactly give her a great deal of confidence, but Hannah reminded herself that it was, after all, only a small leak. Probably a new washer was all that was needed. Besides, it would keep him in another part of the restaurant, safe from the usually good-natured Cal Potter, who'd threatened to take off after Trace with a nail gun if he put another ding in his carefully crafted oak shelving.

"Just change the washer," she instructed. "Don't try anything fancy."

"What's the matter, Hannah, don't you trust me to do the job right?" There was a glint in his eye that could have been either laughter or irritation; she wasn't sure which.

"Of course I do." The truth was that Trace had proven himself a remarkably inept handyman.

Trace grinned at her blatant lie. "I'll call if I get in over my head."

Hannah found herself smiling as she watched him saunter away. He'd changed his uniform for a wool shirt, worn at the elbows, and a pair of low-slung jeans as faded as her own. The snug jeans were definitely an improvement over his khaki uniform trousers, she decided. Then, with a shake of her head, she reminded herself of the miles of pantry shelves that still needed sanding.

She'd lost track of how long she'd been working. The men had left hours ago. Outside, a harvest moon was rising, bathing Mingus Mountain in a blood-red glow that was almost otherworldly. Immersed in her work, Hannah had actually forgotten about Trace. Until she heard him call her name from the rest room.

"Uh, Hannah?"

"Gracious," she murmured, putting down her brush, "are you still here?"

"I think I've just about got it."

"I'm glad to hear that." Hannah glanced down at her watch. Sixty minutes, not bad for a simple washer change. Not when it was Trace doing the plumbing, at any rate.

"The thing is, I could use a little help holding the pipes steady while I turn the wrench."

A tingling of trepidation skimmed up her spine. "Pipes?" she asked, heading toward the bathroom immediately. "Trace, all I asked you to do was—"

She broke off as she stood in the doorway, staring down at the long booted legs. Trace was lying on his back on the floor, his head inside the new oak vanity Cal had installed just yesterday. "What on earth?"

"I replaced the washer, like you suggested," he explained, "but then it started dripping even worse. So I decided that the problem is in this joint right here, but the damn thing is stuck, and—" He hit the handle of the pipe wrench with the palm of his hand. Once. Twice. Then once again. "Damn!"

Without warning, a flood of water burst out of the pipe like a miniature Niagara Falls, drenching Trace. Sitting up too quickly, he slammed his head against the bottom of the cast-iron sink. The water kept coming. When he shouted a string of virulent curses, Hannah raced outside and turned off the water at the source.

He was struggling to his feet when she returned to the bathroom. "Who the hell turned the water back on?" he roared, accepting the towel she handed him without a word of thanks.

His hair was plastered down, water trailed down his angry face, his clothes were clinging wetly to his body. He looked wonderful.

"I'm afraid that was me," she admitted.

"You?" Trace stared at her unbelievingly. "You knew I was working in there, Hannah."

"Yes. Well, you see, I thought everyone had gone, and I wanted to make a pot of decaf, so I had to turn the water back on, and—"

Trace stopped her by holding up his hand. "You forgot I was here?"

"Not exactly. I mean, if I'd thought about it, I would have realized that I hadn't said good-night to you when the others left. But I got busy, and you just sort of slipped my mind."

Trace stared at her. "I slipped your mind?"

From the stunned expression on his handsome face, Hannah had the feeling that were she to glance down at the vinyl tile floor, she'd see Trace's male ego lying in tatters.

"That's not what I meant to say," she hastened to assure him. Walking disaster or not, he'd given up his evenings to help her. Surely that deserved some special handling. "What I meant was that, after the others left, I got lost in my work, and—"

"Forgot all about me," he put in glumly.

Hannah was feeling more and more like the Wicked Witch of the West. "Not exactly," she murmured, twisting her fingers together in front of her.

Trace's wet chest rose and fell as he exhaled a long suffering sigh. "No. That's exactly what you meant, Hannah. You forgot all about me."

"Oh, Trace," she murmured, taking the towel from his hands and looping it around his neck, "you couldn't be any more wrong."

Looking slightly encouraged, Trace put his hands on her hips. "You did forget me."

"If that's the case, and I'm not saying it is," she insisted softly, "it's partly your fault."

"My fault?" He drew her closer. Hannah could feel the tingling and the aching spreading through her body.

"You haven't exactly pressed your case."

"Are you telling me that after I've spent all this time trying to prove to you that I'm interested in more than your body, you're mad because I haven't been trying to tumble you in the sawdust every chance I get?"

"I'm not mad."

"Hurt?"

"No. Not hurt, either."

"How about disappointed?"

She pressed a hand to his chest. "Perhaps. Just a little."

It was all the encouragement Trace needed. He pulled her against him, letting her feel the heat, the passion, through the dampness of his jeans. Rubbing against him with a slow, primitive rhythm, Hannah was amazed that they weren't surrounded by clouds of steam.

"I have wanted you," he insisted against her mouth.

Hannah thrust her fingers through his hair, fitting herself even more closely, if that were possible, to his body. His heart—or hers, she couldn't tell them apart—was pounding. "Really?"

"Really. Remember last night when I left for a while?"

"I remember." He promised he'd be back, and against her will, she'd found herself watching for his Jeep to drive up in front of the cafe.

"I had to go home and take a cold shower."

She tilted her head back to look up at him. "You're kidding."

"Nope." His fingers brushed her neck, creating a trail of tiny shivers. "It was either that or have my way with you on top of that pile of Sheetrock."

"Sheetrock is awfully hard."

His tongue flicked into her ear, then retreated. "I have a difficult time believing we'd even notice."

"Still," Hannah protested in a passion-choked whisper, "if we're going to make love, Trace, I'd think a bed would be preferable."

His hands had been cupping her bottom; his lips had been playing over the silken skin behind her ear. At her words, Trace grew suddenly very still.

"Are you saying what I think you're saying?"

She felt as if she were teetering on the edge of a towering cliff. Taking a deep breath that should have calmed, but didn't, Hannah plunged into the swirling waters below. "Mrs. MacGregor isn't expecting me home for another hour."

An hour wasn't much when you wanted an eternity, Trace considered. Then again, compared to another night of icy showers, it was an aeon.

"If that's the case," he said, punctuating his words with kisses, "why are we wasting time standing around here?"

THE NIGHT WAS CLEAR, tinged with a promise of the winter soon to come. By the time Hannah walked up to the front door of Trace's two-story, white clapboard house, the crisp air had cleared her head, forcing her to view her behavior free from the sensual cloud that had been fogging her mind.

Oh, she wanted him. There'd been too many times over the past weeks that she'd imagined this moment, fantasized about it while tossing and turning in her lonely bed late at night. It had been more than eighteen months since she'd had sex; it only stood to reason that as her grief over David's death faded, other emotions, other needs, would begin to surface.

She was a normal, healthy woman, approaching her sexual peak. And Trace was a sexy, impossibly handsome man. Her feelings for him were entirely natural, Hannah reassured herself. In fact, she'd probably have something to worry about if she didn't want him.

But want was an uncomplicated emotion—easily felt and just as easily satiated. What worried Hannah was that her feelings for Trace Murphy were more complicated than mere desire. Try as she might, she couldn't quite shake the terrible misgiving that if—when—she did go to bed with him, she'd end up giving too much.

To Trace's amazement, his own emotions were far from calm. He'd been waiting for this moment for days. Weeks. Since he'd first discovered the Widow Greene was years younger and worlds more appealing than expected. He hadn't been lying about the showers; there had been too many occasions when he'd been forced to stand for long, uncomfortable minutes under the icy spray, trying to cool down erotic fantasies that had sprung unbidden into his mind.

In the beginning, it had come as a shock to Trace how Hannah had managed to infiltrate every corner of his mind. She was never out of his thoughts, appearing to him in myriad sensual poses. He envisioned making love to her in front of a crackling fire, under a canopy of stars, in the wide canopied bed where three generations of young Murphy brides had given up their innocence.

There was no denying that he wanted her with a need that bordered on obsession. But Trace had been in love before. And that love, albeit too short-lived, was what allowed him to realize that something else might be happening between him and Hannah. Something he didn't want to destroy before he had a chance to explore it further.

When they entered the living room, a large dalmatian lifted his head and eyed Hannah with interest.

"This must be the marvelous Merlin," she guessed.

"In the flesh. He'd get up and greet you properly, but your son wore him out this afternoon playing fetch the handcuffs."

"Hello, boy." Hannah bent down to pat the large spotted head. Merlin thumped his tail happily on the rug. "I hope Scott wasn't too much of a nuisance."

"Not at all. In fact, I've been meaning to talk to you about paying him for exercising Merlin every day."

"That's not necessary. If you want to get technical, I should be paying you for baby-sitting services."

They'd been over this before. Each time Hannah had brought it up, Trace had steadfastly refused. "Why don't we just call it even. For now," he suggested easily.

Hannah nodded as she straightened. "For now."

A slightly uncomfortable silence settled between them. That she was nervous was obvious. Trace watched the telltale signs: her hands twisting together, the way her gray eyes darted around the living room like frightened birds, never lighting anywhere.

"Would you like to sit down?" he asked, gesturing toward the leather sofa.

"No, thank you." She was standing in the center of the room, as if on the verge of running away.

"How about a drink?"

She forced a smile. "I don't think so."

Trace was rapidly coming to the conclusion that he should have gone ahead and made love to Hannah on the Sheetrock. Because the mood was rapidly slipping out of his grasp.

"Would you like to talk?"

She looked at him with surprise. "Talk?"

"Yeah, you know, as in having a conversation. That's where you talk, then I talk, then the ball's back in your court. I'm told some people manage to go on like that for several minutes. Sometimes even hours."

As many times as Hannah had fantasized about making love to Trace Murphy, never had the scenario included conversation. "What would we talk about?"

"Anything you'd like. The Red Rock . . ."

"Just for one hour, I'd like to forget about that place," Hannah muttered.

"Done. We could talk about the weather."

"Hal Potter says that according to his *Farmer's Almanac*, we're in for a long, cold winter."

The image of making love to Hannah in front of a warm, crackling fire while snow fell outside flashed once again in front of his eyes. "That doesn't count. Hal's an electrician, not a farmer."

"Ah, but how does that explain the caterpillar?"

"Caterpillar?"

"The one Fred gave Scott."

"Fred Wiley gave Scott a caterpillar?" When he experienced something akin to jealousy, Trace told himself that Hannah really was driving him crazy.

"A fat, furry, orange and black one. According to Fred, something about the stripes—I forgot exactly what— forecast a long winter."

"Well, that settles it. You just can't argue with a cater-pillar. Sure you don't want something to drink?"

For a moment, Hannah had begun to relax and enjoy herself. Trace's innocent question reminded her of her reason for being here. "No, really, I think I'd better not." This time her attempt at a smile faltered badly. When she dragged her left hand nervously through her hair, Trace caught the unmistakable glint of gold.

Spanning the gap between them, he caught her trem-bling hand in his. "You don't have to be afraid of me, Hannah."

She swallowed past the lump in her throat. "I'm not afraid."

Unconvinced, he brushed his fingertip over her knuck-les. "Aren't you?" he asked quietly. When he began toying with the slim gold band, he could feel her slight tremor.

"No."

Dragging her eyes away from his concerned gaze, she stared unseeingly down at the floor. Merlin, who thought she was looking at him, began thumping his tail encour-agingly. Neither Hannah nor Trace noticed.

"I think I'm afraid of me. Of how I feel." A small, re-gretful sigh escaped before she could prevent it, a sigh that told him more than words ever could. "I really do want you," she whispered.

"I know." It took an effort, but Trace kept his tone from revealing exactly how much he'd like to throw Hannah over his shoulder and carry her into his bedroom. There he'd toss her onto Grandmother Murphy's wedding-ring quilt, strip off all her clothes and spend the rest of the night making mad, passionate love to her until they were both too tired and too satiated to move. "I also know how much you loved your husband," he said quietly.

Stunned at the mention of David during a conversation that had begun as a prelude to lovemaking, Hannah instinctively recoiled.

Not wanting to let her get away until he'd gotten this off his chest, Trace cupped her shoulders comfortingly with his palms. "I'd never ask you to deny what you and David had together, Hannah. Because it's obvious that your marriage was special."

"Trace, really," Hannah protested, "I don't think this is the time or the place—"

"That's where you're wrong." He spoke in a quiet, yet unmistakably authoritative voice, reminding her that he was undoubtedly accustomed to people obeying him without question. "If we don't talk about him now, he'll always be there between us."

"David isn't standing between us," she insisted, not quite truthfully.

"Isn't he?" Before she could deny his softly spoken accusation, his next words came as a complete surprise. "You've never asked about my marriage."

"I didn't think it any of my business."

"I think it is," he quietly corrected her. "Ellen and I grew up together—she lived on the neighboring ranch."

"The neighboring ranch?" Hannah questioned. "But that would make her—"

"Jake Brennan's daughter," he confirmed.

No wonder Jake and Trace were so close, Hannah realized. "How did she..." She couldn't make herself say the word. "What happened?"

"We'd been married six months when she flew up to Denver to visit a friend from college who'd just had a baby. On the way back, a freak winter storm came up and the plane somehow went off course and ended up flying into the side of Mingus Mountain." He scrubbed his hand over his face, as if to expunge the bitter memory. "I headed up the search party that found the wreckage. There weren't any survivors."

Moved beyond words, Hannah pressed her palm against the side of his face. "I'm sorry."

"So was I. Ellen and I had been your quintessential high-school sweethearts. From the time I was old enough to decide that girls were a lot more fun than duck hunting, I figured she and I would be spending the rest of our lives together."

His look was immeasurably solemn. "I didn't tell you this so you'd feel sorry for me, Hannah. I told you about Ellen so you'd understand that I know what you're going through. I loved my wife. And although we weren't married nearly as long as you and David, I value the time we did have together. I also want you to realize that your love for your husband only makes you more special to me."

"How?"

He caught both her hands in his and lifted them to his lips. "Because all those years with David have contributed to the woman you are today." His smile was like a ray of warm summer sunshine, banishing any clouds that might have been lingering overhead. "And believe me, sweetheart, you are one extraordinary lady."

Over the past weeks, Hannah had come to realize that Trace was more than a sexy, desirable male. He was a genuinely kind and gentle man. She could only hope he was also a patient and forgiving one.

"Oh, Trace, you're going to think I'm a horrible person."

He could still have her, Trace knew. Despite her renewed vacillation, he knew that with a single kiss, a lingering caress, he could have her in his bed, her long, silken legs wrapped around his hips, begging him to take her. But then what? Trace asked himself. What of tomorrow?

As he tipped her downcast chin up with his fingertip and saw the confusion in her eyes, Trace was stunned to realize that he wanted a lifetime of tomorrows with Hannah.

"Never," he vowed in a husky voice that was not as steady as it might have been.

Hannah heard the ragged note and mistook it for unsatisfied desire. She took hold of his arms, feeling his strength, knowing instinctively that a woman would feel safe in these arms. Protected. It was that, more than anything else about Trace that frightened her. Trace Murphy was a man accustomed to being in charge. Would he really be happy with an independent woman?

And even more importantly, would she be happy returning to the passive, protected woman she used to be? Hannah had come too far to allow herself to retreat to the security of a man's protection just because things had gotten a little rough.

"It's just that I need a little more time." Just until the Red Rock opened, Hannah told herself. Then, as soon as she was standing fully on her own two feet, she'd be able to handle an affair with Trace without getting in over her head.

Without taking his eyes from hers, Trace lifted her hand to his lips and pressed a kiss against her palm. When he caressed the tender skin with the tip of his tongue—slowly, lingeringly—a jolt of passion arced between her thighs. Satisfied by the vivid response he saw in her startled gaze, Trace lowered her hand to her side.

"How about some hot spiced cider?" he asked with an extraordinary amount of calm, considering his aroused body was throbbing with unrequited need.

Every cell in her body was on red alert; every instinct she had told her to give in to temptation and make love to Trace now, if only to cool the fires raging inside her. She could always worry about regaining her hard-earned independence in the morning. Struggling against dual desires of mind and body, she forced herself to listen to reason.

"I really should leave. Mrs. MacGregor will be anxious to get home."

"You said she wasn't expecting you for an hour," he reminded her. "Come on, Hannah, what can it hurt? We'll share a little cider, talk a little, then I'll walk you home."

It certainly sounded harmless enough. Hannah thought about how long it had been since she'd just relaxed and enjoyed herself with another adult. Scott was a terrific little boy, and she adored her only son, but try as he might, he couldn't take the place of his father. Not that she wanted Trace in that role, either, she assured herself.

"I think I'd like that," she agreed finally.

Trace's victorious grin suggested that he'd never expected any other outcome. "Terrific. Make yourself at home and I'll be right back." He bent down, brushed a quick, unthreatening kiss against her forehead, then left the room.

"I'll probably regret this," Hannah said to Merlin as she sank down onto the sofa. "But your master is difficult to resist."

Happy to finally be included in the conversation, Merlin rose from the rug and ambled over to her, tail wagging happily like a metronome set for presto. As she patted the polka-dot head the dog had thrust under her hand, Hannah decided that to describe Trace as difficult to resist was an understatement.

He was impossible to resist. And the more time Hannah spent in his company, the more she wondered why a woman would even want to try.

8

THE CIDER WAS HOT, fragrantly spiced and, coming after a long day's work, definitely appreciated. As she sipped it slowly in front of the crackling fire, Hannah gradually relaxed.

"Who carved the menagerie?" she asked, picking up an intricately detailed wooden antelope from the coffee table.

"That was me."

"You?"

He chuckled. "Surprised?"

She ran a finger over the smooth wood. The antelope was incredibly lifelike, as were all the other animals scattered about the room. "Let's just say that you've kept your woodworking skills well hidden."

"You've forgotten about my potato peeling."

"That's right," she recalled, "you said something about pretending you were whittling."

"I may be a klutz with a hammer or a wrench, but my grandfather was a world-class whittler. I used to spend a lot of summer evenings sitting on the front porch, watching him bring a piece of wood to life. I suppose it only figures I'd pick up some of his tricks."

"They're lovely," she murmured, replacing the antelope on the table.

"Thanks."

"You know, I really do like your house," she murmured, glancing around the cozy, homey room.

Two of the four walls were distressed wooden planks that she took to be barn siding. The fireplace had been fashioned out of the same red rocks from which the Red Rock Café had been constructed; the rugged furniture was a lustrous antiqued pine that had been hand-rubbed and distressed for a rich and mellow look.

It was a room designed for comfort and quiet relaxation. But it was still a man's room and Hannah couldn't resist mentally adding a few touches—a row of stenciling along the top of the unpaneled walls, a copper bed-warmer hanging beside the fireplace, pewter mugs on the mantel and some green plants hanging in the window.

"The paneling's from Dad's old barn," he said.

"I thought it might be." She sipped on the cider. "That's a nice way of keeping in touch with your past."

"My grandfather built that barn, with the help of his neighbors, the weekend before he married my grandmother. Since he didn't have enough money to buy the lumber for both a house and a barn, they spent the first six months of their marriage camping out in the hayloft."

Hannah looked at him suspiciously. "Is that true?"

"Of course. Fortunately, they managed to get a one-room cabin built before winter set in." He flashed her one of those quick grins she was finding more and more difficult to resist. "Although we Murphy men are renowned for our lovemaking skills, I'm not certain even Grandpa Murphy could've kept Grandma warm all the time, once the temperatures dipped down into single digits."

"Is the cabin still standing?"

"Sure is. Except now it's the guest bedroom in my dad's ranch house. Granddad, and then Dad, just kept adding rooms as they needed them," he explained at her questioning look.

"It must have been nice," she mused aloud, "growing up surrounded by so much tradition."

Trace shrugged. "I guess I never gave it a lot of thought. Just about everyone in town is descended from the original settlers."

"Cal mentioned that your great-great-grandfather founded the town."

"Yeah. Jedidiah Murphy was the third son of a Boston lawyer and politician, who eschewed the political life that was the family tradition and become a librarian."

"A librarian?"

"A librarian," he confirmed. "Jedidiah was well-educated, highly respected, and definitely the least adventuresome of the three brothers. That's why everyone was so surprised when he suddenly packed everything he and my great-great-grandmother owned into a wagon and headed off to California, where he promptly came down with a near-fatal case of gold fever."

"I think I can figure out where the idea of all the Murphy men being crazy started."

He grinned good-naturedly. "Heard that one, have you?"

"Jake told me." Hannah didn't mention that not only had Cal and Fred Wiley offered a similar appraisal, Mitzi had mentioned it as well. "Tell me more about Jedidiah."

"Well, according to the stories, the first two claims he bought from speculators turned out to be salted."

"Salted?"

"It was an old trick pulled by the precursors of modern land-developers. They'd sprinkle a little gold dust on the bottom of the creek so they could sell the claim for an exaggerated value to unsuspecting greenhorns. Poor Jedidiah was a trusting soul. It took him a while to catch on."

"And when he did?"

"Sure was. When no more gold was found, the settlement became known as Murphy's Folly. Finally, the miners moved on to greener—or golder, as the case may be— pastures, leaving behind others who'd come to enjoy the way of life they'd found here."

"The new chance," she murmured.

He smiled down at her. "Exactly."

"That's why I came," she admitted.

Trace's only response was an arched brow.

"I fell in love with the name the moment I saw it in the paper," she explained quietly. "It had been a horrible day. I'd spent the morning with the IRS trying to arrange payment for the back taxes David owed on his business, and that afternoon I'd met with the broker who was going to list the house, and the auctioneer who was going to sell off my furniture. I returned home, almost overwhelmed by a feeling of quiet desperation when I opened the *Wall Street Journal* and saw Mitzi's ad."

"Advertising the Red Rock."

She smiled at the memory. "I don't even remember what the ad said. All I saw were the words New Chance. It was like fate."

Grinning, Trace skimmed his finger down her nose. "What if you'd known fate came with a life-size steer on top of its roof?"

"I still would have come."

"And now?" he questioned, forcing his tone to remain casual.

"Now?" He was suddenly so close. Had he moved? Or had she?

"Are you glad you've come?"

Their eyes met and held for what seemed an eternity. Hannah knew that they were no longer talking about the

Red Rock, but something far more important. "Very," she whispered finally.

He brushed his smiling lips against hers. "I'm glad."

His breath was warm, spiced, reminding her of autumn in New England. When he would have lifted his head, Hannah framed his face with her hands, continuing the kiss, deepening it until she felt the greedy, answering heat of his mouth all the way down to her toes, which were curling in her sneakers.

It was Trace who finally broke away. "I'd better be seeing you home," he said in a choked voice.

Hannah's head was still spinning; her body ached, her lips tingled. "Yes," she whispered, although she meant no.

Rising unsteadily to her feet, she was appalled to discover her legs had about as much substance as warm Jello. If Trace Murphy could create such weakness from a mere kiss, she was almost afraid to think what would happen were she ever to give in to impulse and make love to him. She'd probably melt from the intense heat of it.

Unfolding his length from the leather sofa, Trace stood in front of her, not bothering to conceal his arousal. As she watched his body straining against the faded denim, Hannah had an urge to reach out and press her palm against the bold outline. That idea swiftly brought another, even more outrageous than its predecessor, and she had to struggle against the sudden desire to drop to her knees and press her lips against the taut, bulging denim. A small, desperate mew escaped her lips.

"Poor Hannah," Trace murmured, reading the undisguised desire in her eyes, "this isn't turning out to be as easy as it should be, is it?"

"It is difficult," she admitted falteringly, dragging her eyes back up to his face. "It seems like we're never alone, and then, when we are—"

"We're racing the clock."

She nodded.

He held her by the elbows, close enough that she could feel the heat radiating from his body. "What would you say to going away together?"

Hannah stared up at him blankly. "Going away? With you? Where?"

He'd been trying to come up with a way to ask her for two weeks, but every time he'd approached her, he'd felt like a tongue-tied adolescent. "There's an Arizona Law Enforcement Awards banquet and dance in Phoenix tomorrow night," he said quickly, before he chickened out once again. "I have to attend. I thought you might like a night off from the Red Rock."

A night off sounded like nirvana. A night off with Trace sounded even better. "You're getting an award, aren't you?"

To her amazement, a dark red flush rose from the neck of his wool shirt. "Yeah," he mumbled. "I guess I am."

Pride warred with embarrassment in his face, reminding her of Scott, the day he'd won the second-grade spelling bee. Hannah found his behavior endearing.

"What for?"

"I don't recall the exact wording. Something about valor in the field."

Hannah knew that had she been receiving the award, she would have memorized every word. "Congratulations. You must be very proud."

He shrugged, appearing more uncomfortable by the moment. "I didn't really do anything. After all it's—"

"If you dare try to tell me that valor is merely part of the job, I'll pick up that poker and hit you over the head, Trace Murphy," Hannah threatened heatedly.

Trace decided that he liked Hannah's flare of temper. An angry woman was not an indifferent one. "Yes ma'am," he said, repressing a grin.

Hannah studied him intently, suspecting that he was laughing at her. When his green eyes appeared absolutely guileless, she nodded her satisfaction. "That's better. And I'd be honored to watch you receive your award, Trace. How late should I tell Mrs. MacGregor we'll be getting back?"

Well, it was now or never, Trace decided. He cleared his throat. "What would you say if I said Saturday, around noon?"

"You want me to spend the night with you?"

That was precisely what he wanted. It was what he'd been wanting since that first day. Since she walked into the Red Rock Café looking like an angel and smelling of wild-flowers. "Not *with* me," he felt obliged to say, "we'd have separate hotel rooms."

"Phoenix is only two hours away. Why stay in a hotel at all?"

"Because these award dinners always run long. And if we stay for the dancing, we probably wouldn't leave until one or two, and quite frankly, I'd just as soon not drive when I'm that tired."

It made a certain amount of sense, she considered.

"The hotel's offering reduced rates for anyone who wants to stay over," he went on. "It's something they started doing in order to reduce the number of drunk drivers on the highways." Unable to resist touching her, he reached out and brushed his fingertips over her nape. "Say yes, Hannah."

"I suppose I could ask Mrs. MacGregor to spend the night."

Trace hoped that the decided lack of enthusiasm in her
voice was due to her unwillingness to supply the nosy Mrs.
MacGregor with such a succulent piece of gossip. "Or
Scott could stay out at the ranch with Dad," he suggested. "He seemed to enjoy himself on Thanksgiving."

"He had a great time. All he's talked about for days is
that horse your dad let him ride."

"Rusty's a patient old thing," Trace assured her. "You
needn't worry about Scott getting hurt."

"I wasn't worried about that."

"Then what's the problem?"

"Surely your father has better things to do than baby-
sit an eight-year-old boy," she protested, thinking of Dan
and Mitzi's romance.

Trace took both her hands in his. "Hannah, Dad came
up with the idea of Scott staying with him last week. He
wouldn't have made the offer if he didn't honestly enjoy
having Scott there."

"You talked about this with him last week?"

"Yes."

"But you didn't discuss it with me until this evening."

"That's right."

"You should get a second medal, Trace."

"Second medal?" He didn't like the way her eyes had
frosted over.

"For egotism above and beyond the call of duty," she
snapped.

Trace's fingers tightened on hers, forestalling her effort
to retrieve her hands. "What the hell does that mean?"

"It means that just because I don't currently have a man
in my life, that doesn't mean that I'm just sitting around,
dying to have you ask me out at the last minute!"

He stared at her for a long time. Incensed that he'd take her so for granted, Hannah glared back at him. When he threw back his head and began to laugh, she seethed.

"I'm glad you find my feelings so humorous," she muttered.

"You've got it all wrong."

She tilted her chin in a way that made Trace want to kiss her all the more. "I do?"

"You do." His look brimmed over with good-natured affection. "The truth is, sweetheart, that I didn't ask you earlier because I was terrified you'd turn me down."

The very thought was stunning in its implication. Hannah wondered if Trace could possibly feel as unnerved by their relationship as she. Impossible, she told herself firmly.

"Really?" she heard herself asking.

"Really." He lifted her hands and put them around his neck. Encouraged when she allowed them to stay there, he looped his arms around her waist. "I know you'll find this hard to believe, Hannah, but ever since you arrived in New Chance, I've been feeling horribly, excruciatingly like I did in high school."

As she stood face-to-face with him, Hannah found herself entranced by the slow, simmering flame in his emerald eyes. "No," she said softly. "I don't find that difficult to believe at all."

Without taking his eyes from hers, Trace ran his knuckles down her cheek. "You, too?"

His tender touch, his warming gaze, were too enticing for words. Hannah closed her eyes with a slow, accepting blink. "Me, too."

Trace felt like belting out the Hallelujah Chorus. "So, how about it?" he asked instead. "Wanna salvage what's left of my ego by letting me take the prettiest girl in New Chance to the prom?"

"With a line like that," she said with an answering smile, "how could I resist?"

"I REALLY CAN'T afford to do this," Hannah protested the following morning as Mitzi dragged her through what appeared to be every boutique in nearby Sedona.

"Pooh, you can't afford not to," the older woman protested, rifling through the racks with the skill of a veteran shopper. "Did Cinderella go to the ball in her everyday rags? What do you think of this?" she asked, holding up a strapless scarlet satin dress with a short bell skirt.

Hannah tried not to be offended by the fact that Mitzi had referred to her usual clothing as rags. "I think that even if I could keep it up, which I couldn't, I'd freeze to death before we got to the main course. And if I recall the story, Cinderella had a fairy godmother to pay the bill for those glass slippers."

"So do you. How about this one?" The emerald silk was closer to what Hannah had in mind, if she *had* been looking for a dress, which she wasn't, she reminded herself. But it still wasn't quite right.

"Green makes me look sallow. What do you mean, so do I?"

Mitzi ignored her pointed question. "Black is always nice," she mused, lingering over a short black cocktail dress.

"I'd feel like I was wearing widow's weeds. And you still haven't answered my question."

"I forgot about the widow thing," Mitzi apologized, sifting through the racks. "Bingo."

Even as Hannah opened her mouth to reiterate the fact that she wasn't in the market for a new dress, she drew in

"He got a stake from a man he'd met in a poker game and went out on his own. Six months later, he'd struck it rich."

Hannah smiled. After such a run of bad luck as she'd had, she was pleased to hear of the good fortunes of others. "I'm glad."

Trace had slid his arm around her shoulder and his fingers were playing idly with the ends of her hair. "The only problem was, the word got out before he got back to town and when he arrived at the recording office, he discovered the guy who'd staked him had already filed a claim."

"I don't believe it! He was cheated again?"

"According to family legend, that's just about the same thing my great-great-grandmother said. She convinced him that he didn't belong in the California gold fields, that he was too naive, too trusting. All the rascals and scoundrels could see him coming a mile away."

"Sounds as if great-great-grandmother Murphy was a clever woman."

"She was a firecracker. You would have loved her. Anyway," Trace continued, "she and Jedidiah packed what was left of their belongings back onto the wagon and headed east to Arizona where there'd been a rumor of a gold strike on Oak Creek, up around where Sedona is today."

"But he never got there?"

"Nope. He and Mary were camping out along the river, right where Dad's ranch is today, when he spotted a gold nugget gleaming in the water. He staked a claim, which immediately brought others, swelling the population of the settlement Jedidiah was calling New Chance to over five thousand."

"That's more than today."

a quick, sudden breath. The cocktail gown Mitzi had pulled from the rack was without a doubt one of the most beautiful she'd ever seen. Fashioned from silk, in a shade that was neither gold, nor bronze, but some gleaming color in between, it looked like autumn fire.

"How much?" she asked with a deep sigh.

Mitzi plucked the coded tag from the dress. "It doesn't matter," she said blithely, stuffing the dress into Hannah's arms. "Go try it on."

"Not until I know how much it costs."

Mitzi's frustrated sigh ruffled her dyed-gold bangs. "For heaven's sake, Hannah, it doesn't matter. Because I'm paying for it."

Hannah's mouth dropped open. "I can't let you do that," she protested, once she'd found her voice again.

"Of course you can. Go try it on while I look for a suitable evening bag."

"Mitzi—"

"Look," the older woman said, "tonight's a big night for you and Trace. Call me an unabashed romantic, if you will, but I want it to be special for both of you."

"Still—"

Mitzi cut her off by holding up her hand. Diamonds sparkled on three of her perfectly manicured fingers. "Look, Hannah, if you want to get down to brass tacks, I owe you that dress. For years after Dan's wife died, he seemed perfectly content to live alone out there at that ranch. Then I came to town, shook up his life a bit, made him feel like a young stud. But, try as I might, I couldn't get him thinking that what we had might grow into something permanent."

"I understand how you feel," Hannah said, "but what does that have to do with you owing me this dress?"

"Watching his son fall so fast and so hard for you has made Dan think more about his own feelings. And Scott— well, your little boy had him considering how much he'd like to be a grandfather, while he's still young enough to enjoy it. And while he was thinking about all that, it finally dawned on the old fool that perhaps he isn't too old to take one more ride on the marriage-go-round."

Hannah stared at her. "Are you telling me . . ."

"He proposed last night," Mitzi revealed. Hannah knew that the satisfied gleam in the woman's eyes had nothing to do with her tinted contacts. "We're getting married on Christmas Eve and I'd love for you to be my matron of honor."

"Oh, I'd love that, too. I'm so happy for you." The dress was crushed between them as Hannah hugged the person who was responsible for bringing her to New Chance in the first place.

"Then do me a favor and let me buy that dress," Mitzi insisted. "If it fits like I think it will, we just might make it a double wedding."

"I'm certainly not planning to get married," Hannah protested.

Mitzi changed gears with the deftness of a natural-born saleswoman. "Of course you're not," she agreed without missing a beat. "But you can't deny that would make a great matron-of-honor dress." She studied the dress judiciously. "Of course the back is cut a little low, you'd have to wear the matching jacket with it." Mitzi flashed Hannah the practiced, appealing smile that never failed to close a deal. "Try on the dress, Hannah. I just know it's going to be dynamite."

"Well, I suppose I could use a new dress for the wedding," she murmured, trailing her hands over the gleaming silk.

Mitzi tilted her gilded head in the direction of the dressing rooms. "Go try it on."

The dress flowed over her body like rippling water cascading down a mountain stream. The short flirty skirt, ideal for dancing, ended at her knees, displaying her long legs to advantage. But it was when she turned around that the dress revealed its full potential: the neckline, which skimmed her collarbone in front, plunged down to her waist in the back, revealing a provocative amount of ivory flesh.

Take that, Trace Murphy, Hannah thought with an inward smile as she considered his predictable reaction. She loved it. She would also never, in a million years, have the nerve to wear it in public without the waist-length, beaded jacket.

"How's it fit?" Mitzi called in to her.

"It's a little snug," Hannah lied, vowing to get out of the dress—and the boutique—before she gave in to temptation and changed her mind.

"Let me see." Entering the dressing room without an invitation, Mitzi whistled under her breath as she stared at Hannah's reflection in the three-way mirror. "Poor Trace. The man's a goner."

"What do you mean?" Hannah asked with feigned innocence, as she turned this way and that, feeling like a young girl playing dress-up for the first time. She was amazed at the magic the dress had performed. She looked . . . almost sexy, she decided.

"One look at you in this, and you're going to have that poor unsuspecting male wrapped around your little finger," Mitzi predicted.

"You make it sound so easy." As she smoothed nonexistent wrinkles from her skirt, Hannah's attention was drawn to her wedding ring. Not for the first time. Hannah felt her courage faltering. "I really did love my husband, Mitzi."

"Of course you did," the older woman said soothingly. "But like it or not, Hannah, David's gone. Did you ever think that perhaps it's time to start living for yourself?"

Hannah's grave gray eyes met Mitzi's sympathetic blue ones in the mirror. "What do you think tonight's all about?"

Mitzi nodded, apparently satisfied. "You slip out of that," she said with renewed briskness. "I'll round up a bag and a pair of shoes." Ignoring Hannah's sputtered protests, she left the dressing room in search of accessories.

Knowing she should be irritated by Mitzi Patterson's overbearing but well-meaning attitude, Hannah simply continued to stare at the sexy stranger in the mirror. Then she smiled.

HANNAH WAS STILL SMILING eight hours later as she slid into the deep hotel bathtub, luxuriating in the warmth of the scented water as it lapped lightly across her stomach and breasts. When she imagined the blue foam to be Trace's exciting, caressing hands, her bones seemed to grow as soft and pliant as the fragrant water.

Her rebellious mind, once stimulated, seemed unable to stop creating erotic pictures and as she checked her reflection for the umpteenth time in the mirror, Hannah was not at all surprised to find that the woman gazing back at her was a woman who very much wanted to be made love to. Feeling outrageously, atypically reckless tonight, she'd left the beaded jacket on its padded hanger in the closet.

The very thought of making love with Trace caused her blood to flow warmer in her veins. By the time he knocked on her door, Hannah felt like pulling him down to the gray

wall-to-wall carpeting and having her way with him here
and now.

"You're late," she said by way of greeting as she opened
the door.

Struck speechless by the vision in front of him, Trace
stared at her. He was wearing a navy suit with a thin pin-
stripe, a white shirt and burgundy tie. Hannah decided
that in its own way, the dark suit was as much of a uniform as the one he wore every day. He also looked just as
good in it as he did his sheriff's uniform. Even better, she
decided, observing the way the snow-white shirt con-
trasted handsomely with his dark skin.

"Trace?"

He shook his head, as if to clear it. "Sorry. What did you
say?"

"I said you were late."

He looked down at his watch. "Actually, I think I'm
early. But I got lonely in my room. Have I told you that
you're the most beautiful woman I've ever seen?"

No one had ever called her beautiful. Not even David,
not even on their wedding day. Up until this moment,
pretty had been her highest accolade. Coloring slightly
under his appreciative gaze, Hannah smoothed the
gleaming silk over her thighs with hands that trembled
ever so slightly. "Really?"

"Really." He continued to stare at her.

Hannah glanced down at the dark green bottle he was
holding in his hand. The other hand held a pair of long-
stemmed tulip glasses. "Is that for us?"

Trace looked blankly at the champagne, as if he'd forgotten its existence. "Oh, yeah. There's an open bar at the
pre-dinner reception, but I thought it might be nice to have
a drink before we go downstairs."

"What a wonderful idea. I'd like that."

"I'm glad."

When he still didn't budge, Hannah felt a surge of heady, feminine power. That she could affect any man this way— but especially one as impossibly handsome as Trace Murphy—was a little overwhelming. It was also wonderful.

"Did you plan on us drinking it in the hallway?"

Dragging his eyes from the lush, silk-covered flare of her hips, Trace blinked. "What?"

"The champagne. Would you like to drink it in my room? Or yours?" She smiled, a warm, womanly smile filled with sensual promise.

"I don't know," he said slowly, his eyes taking a slow, seductive tour of her body. Who would have guessed that the Widow Greene's legs went on forever? "Maybe this wasn't such a hot idea after all."

Reaching down, she took the bottle from his hands. "This is supposed to be a very good year," she said, studying the label.

"Oh, that." He shrugged uncaringly. "I just called down to room service and asked for the best they had.... If I come in right now, Hannah, I might not be able to leave."

She knew the feeling. "What about your award?"

"Award?"

"Poor Trace, the excitement must have affected your mind," she said silkily. "Come inside and we'll see if we can restore your memory in time for the banquet."

Trace had no sooner entered the hotel room and shut the door behind him when the telephone on Hannah's beside table rang. When she turned away to answer it, he was given a weakening view of an amazing expanse of creamy, silken skin. Desire slammed into him.

As she picked up the receiver, Hannah was mentally crossing her fingers that whoever was on the other end wasn't calling about anything important. Having already decided to allow herself this one magical night, she hated the idea of anything spoiling it before it had even begun.

"Hello? Oh, yes, he's here. Just a minute."

"It's for you," she said, turning back to Trace. "It's Cal."

The trouble with being sheriff was that it was an around-the-clock job, Trace considered as he took the receiver from Hannah. People who'd never bother their banker or their doctor on vacation felt perfectly free to track him down with their personal grievances. The fact that he'd appointed Cal deputy six months ago had made little difference; people in New Chance were used to calling on Trace when they had a problem. Just as they'd called on his father and his grandfather.

"This better be good," he growled.

As he listened, responding periodically in monosyllables, Hannah set about opening the bottle. If they were going to have to return to New Chance, she at least wanted a glass of champagne before she left.

"Just a little trouble with Jake," he said as he hung up. "He got drunk again."

"Oh, dear." Hannah's eyes filled with a very real concern as she handed Trace a glass. "And he's been doing so well."

"The government set the date for the auction. I suppose that's what set him off."

"No doubt." Hannah knew all too well how upsetting it was to lose everything you'd worked for. "When is it?"

"December twenty-third."

"You'd think they could have waited until after Christmas."

"You'd think so, wouldn't you," Trace agreed. "Damn, I keep hoping some proof of the payment he swears he made will turn up. If only we had a little more time."

They exchanged a bleak look. "Perhaps I could talk to him," Hannah suggested. "Sometimes it helps to know that someone understands what you're going through."

Trace shrugged. "It sure couldn't hurt. Jake likes you."

"I like him, too."

"Actually, he likes you a lot."

"Really?"

"Yep. He keeps telling me that I'm not good enough for you."

Hannah thought she detected a question in Trace's usually self-assured tone. She smiled at him over the rim of her glass. "Why don't we let me be the judge of that?"

"Good idea. I don't suppose you'd be open to a little personal lobbying."

"Feel free to give it your best shot, Sheriff." An unmistakable invitation sparkled in her eyes, lingered on her smiling lips, bloomed in the soft rose of her cheeks.

Trace wondered what he'd ever done to deserve such luck. "I intend to do exactly that," he said in a voice husky with a hunger too long denied. "I'm sorry I was late."

"You weren't. Not really," Hannah admitted. "I was just getting lonely for you."

"Really?"

"Really. I was tempted to bribe a bellboy for the key to that door between us."

"It wouldn't have done you any good."

Hannah arched an ebony brow. "You think not?"

"Nope. But only because I beat you to it." Trace grinned as he reached into the pocket of his navy suit and pulled out a small brass key.

"Why, Sheriff," she complained with a smile, "what would your constituents say if they knew you were guilty of bribery?"

"One look at you in that dress and they'd understand. Hell, any man with blood still stirring in his veins would probably vote for me twice, just on principle."

"Although I shudder at the thought of compromising the integrity of New Chance's political system, I believe I'll take that as a compliment."

"Good, because that's precisely how I meant it." When she would have lifted the glass to her lips, he caught her wrist. "Since this is the first time off either of us has had in a long time, I'd say a toast is in order."

"A toast?"

His warm gaze triggered evocative memories of last night's kiss. "To us."

At any other time, Hannah would have found his words too dangerous, too threatening. Tonight, she could not think of anything she'd rather drink to.

"To us," she agreed, lifting her glass to his. As the crystal rims chimed, their eyes met and exchanged sensual promises.

THE NEXT TWO HOURS flew by in a blur. Hannah was vaguely aware of meeting a number of individuals, all of whom had nothing but praise for Trace. The hotel was as luxurious as she might have expected, had she given the matter any thought, and she was sure that the meal she'd been served was more than adequate. But it could have been cold franks and burned beans for all she noticed; her attention was riveted on Trace. On the gold hair on his tanned wrists below his starched cuffs as he cut his prime rib, on the way the lines fanned out from his green eyes—attractive creases that deepened when he smiled at her, which was often. And most of all, on the warm, sensual feel of his hand against her back as they swayed slowly to the music after dinner.

"I'm having a wonderful time," she murmured, linking her fingers together behind his neck.

"I'm glad. So am I."

"I'm also quite flattered."

"Flattered?" Trace nuzzled her ear.

"To be in the company of Arizona's Lawman of the Year."

He didn't want to talk about his work. Not now. Not when his body was responding to her closeness. "It's no big deal."

She tilted her head back to look up at him. "Being a hero's no big deal?"

"Heroes come and go."

"You saved that entire family. A mother. And two small children."

"It was a lucky accident. I didn't even know they were being held hostage by that guy when I stopped him for speeding."

"But when you realized what was happening, you rescued them."

"Any officer in this room tonight would have done the same thing, Hannah. It's part—"

Hannah pressed her fingertips against his lips. "Don't you dare say it. Not tonight." She rested her head on his shoulder, sighing happily as their bodies pressed together. "Do you have any idea how many women get a date with a full-fledged hero?"

"I've no idea, having never given the matter any thought."

"Hardly any. I feel just like Lois Lane out on a date with Superman."

"Just don't get your hopes up too high—" he pushed aside her hair, allowing his lips access to her neck "—because I can't leap tall buildings in a single bound."

"I certainly wouldn't expect you to."

"And I'm not stronger than a locomotive."

"Who is?"

"And I'm definitely not faster than a speeding bullet."

"Believe me, Trace, you've no idea how happy I am to hear that."

The devilish, almost lascivious glee in Hannah's eyes made Trace's control, which had been hanging by a thread all evening, suddenly snap. His palms slid lower, pressing her against his aroused body.

"What would you say to slipping away from here and moving this party upstairs?"

Hannah went on her toes and pressed a quick, hard kiss against his lips. "Sheriff, I thought you'd never ask."

9

THE ELEVATOR WAS FILLED with a contingent of ebullient conventioneers, but Trace and Hannah were aware only of one another. With his thumb he stroked the soft skin at the inside of her wrist and her pulse hummed; her soft gray eyes, brimming over with sensual promise, smiled up into his and his blood warmed. His gaze dropped to her lips and lingered, as if recalling the silky texture, the passionate heat. The electricity between them was palpable.

The steel doors finally opened on the sixth floor and Trace and Hannah quickly exited, and the moment they entered the room, he drew her into his arms. As much as she'd wanted him, as long as she'd waited for this moment, fantasized about it, Hannah couldn't prevent herself stiffening when she felt his hard body pressing against hers.

Appearing undeterred by her response, Trace pressed a kiss against the gleaming dark crown of her head. "I meant what I said about wanting your company tonight every bit as much as I want to make love to you, Hannah. So all you have to do is say the word and I'll leave. Now, before things get out of hand."

Although Hannah felt like a fool, she couldn't quite dismiss the fear that had been lurking just below the surface ever since she'd admitted her desire for this man. "I really do want you, Trace."

"But?" His hands moved up and down her bare back, the gesture meant to soothe, rather than excite.

Slowly, reluctantly, Hannah tilted her head back to look up at him. Half expecting understandable frustration, even anger, the gentle patience she saw on his face tore at some delicate fiber deep inside her.

Her throat was dry; her lips had turned to stone. "I'm afraid," she managed to whisper.

"Afraid? Of me?" Hurt ricocheted through him. How could she have misjudged him, not to mention what they had together? "Surely you know I'd never do anything you didn't want to do, Hannah."

How to make him understand something she herself could not quite comprehend? Hannah dragged her hand through the sleek curve of her hair. "I told you before, I'm not afraid of you. It's me."

Trace was doing his best to understand. But though he tried to be an understanding, sympathetic man of the eighties, the truth was that, to him, the female mind seemed a complicated and often convoluted thing, and Hannah's was proving no exception. "Are you saying you're afraid of what you feel for me? Of what we have together?"

"No. Well, yes, in a way. I mean, sometimes I worry that we've rushed into things, but that's not what I mean right now." Terrific, Hannah thought, talk about destroying the mood. By the time she finished over-analyzing things, Trace would probably choose a cold shower over making love to her.

Trace combed his fingers through the dark silk of her hair, smoothing the tangles her trembling fingers had left behind. "Sweetheart, I'm honestly trying to understand, but—"

"I'm afraid I'll disappoint you," she blurted out. Mortified by her bald admission, she buried her face in the hard line of his shoulder.

There was a long, shocked silence as Trace stared down at her. Finally, with gentle fingers, he tilted her face up to his. "You could never disappoint me, Hannah," he said gravely.

She could feel the rebellious tears stinging the back of her lids. Resolutely, she blinked them away. "You don't understand. I was a nineteen-year-old virgin when I married David. I'm thirty-three now."

"So?"

"So I've only made love to one man in my entire life." Treacherously close to letting the tears flow, Hannah drew in a deep, shuddering breath. "What if I don't know how to satisfy you? What if I can't please you?" She closed her eyes briefly. When she opened them, Trace could see unmasked dread in their depths. "I'd hate that."

Her arms, which had been linked around his waist, dropped to her sides. Trace lifted her hands to his lips and kissed her palms. Her skin had turned to ice, but he could feel her pulse race at the inside of her wrist and was encouraged. Also encouraging was the fact that she was no longer wearing her wedding ring.

"Sweetheart, you could never displease me." With his large hands he set about gently soothing the rigid knots in her shoulder muscles.

Tension fled, to be replaced by the slow, simmering desire Hannah felt whenever Trace touched her, looked at her. "That's what you say now." Her voice was as breathless as a giddy schoolgirl's. What was the matter with her? No man—not even David, whom she'd adored—had ever made her breathless.

"That's what I say now." He kept his touch tender when what he wanted to do was pull her down onto that inviting wide bed and ravish her body like a wild man. He bent his head and kissed her brow. "And that's what I'll say to-morrow. Forever."

Forever. The word spelled commitment, control. Hesitating, Hannah looked up at him, seeing the truth in his eyes and decided that autonomy no longer seemed essential. Tomorrow morning would come soon enough; she could set about regaining her independence then. For now, for this one glorious night, she was going to follow her heart.

With a soft sigh of surrender, she allowed her eyelids to flutter closed and waited for his kiss, surprised when he touched his lips to her cheek instead.

"I think I could easily get addicted to the taste of your skin," he murmured as his mouth trailed around her jaw to her other cheek, studiously avoiding her slightly parted lips. He was leading her toward the bed, even as he continued to brush soft, tantalizing kisses up the side of her face.

Her lips were stinging with an almost desperate need to be touched. "Trace," she whispered as his mouth loitered hotly at her temple, "kiss me."

"I am." He nibbled lightly on her earlobe and felt her slight shudder. "Turn around."

So desperate was she to feel his mouth on her, so much did she long for another of those slow, deep kisses that took her breath away and caused her heart to treble its beat, Hannah knew that tonight she'd be unable to refuse Trace anything. Trembling with anticipation, she allowed him to turn her slowly in his arms.

Her exposed back shone like porcelain in the muted light, but Trace knew her flesh, framed by the gleaming silk, would be soft and warm. "I've been going crazy, wanting to do this all night," he murmured as he lowered his head.

Hannah caught her breath as his mouth touched her. His tongue slid down her spine to where the satin of her skin gave way to silk, then back again, and a thrill of excitement shot through her. When she would have turned back to him, Trace's wide hands spanned her hips, holding her still as he continued to seduce her with his mouth alone.

His lips skimmed the delicate bones of her spine, his tongue gathered in the perfumed warmth of her skin. Pushing the dress aside, he pressed a gathering of moist, open-mouthed kisses into the small of her back, eliciting soft, ragged sounds of pleasure.

This was how he wanted her, he thought with rising desire, warm, pliant, holding nothing back. If only for tonight.

Tomorrow, when they returned to New Chance, she could be the brisk, efficient restaurateur, rebuilding her life the way she was renovating a century-old building. But for now, for this single night, he wanted to know that he could make her as crazy as she'd been making him.

Maintaining a rigid self-restraint he'd never known he possessed, Trace forced himself to go slowly. Where his lips played, Hannah burned. Where his breath warmed, she ached. When he lifted her hair and lightly nipped her neck, she trembled from the thrill of it. Just when she thought she'd go mad with desire, he turned her in his arms and she looked up to see her own unbridled passion mirrored in his eyes. Their lips met—finally, she thought, almost overwhelmed with relief—and lingered, for a long, luxurious time. Then, without a word, they began undressing each other.

As they lay facing each other on the wide, king-size bed, Hannah's hands skimmed the planes and hollows of Trace's body, her fingers tracing long, corded muscles that contracted under her exploring touch. In turn, Trace moved his hands over her slender curves, drawing out a slow, smoldering pleasure until she thought she'd faint.

Hannah's breathing grew heavy. The soft sounds she made when his lips tugged at the rosy crest of her breast caused a fire to burn in his loins, but still Trace waited. His mouth loitered at the inside of her thigh. When his long, dark fingers drew slow, tantalizing circles through the soft curls between her legs, Hannah arched her body in a bow of utter abandon.

Still he waited.

"So beautiful," he murmured, lifting his head to give her a long, heated look. "I love the way you feel in my arms. I love touching you here . . ." his callused fingers caressed her breasts, "and here . . ." Hannah gasped as his palm pressed against her stomach before moving lower.

Trace watched the need rise in her eyes and felt an answering hunger quicken inside him. "And here . . ." His fingers found the tingling nub, causing it to flame under his caresses.

"Trace . . . please." His touch had set off an inferno of sensations; every nerve ending in her body was concentrated on that one, vital, quivering spot.

Her mind was spinning. Before she could anticipate it, Trace lowered his head and kissed her and pleasure exploded like fireworks inside her.

At her delighted cry of surprise, Trace's control snapped and he surged into her, thrusting deeply, again and again, the blood pounding in his veins until he thought he'd explode from the force of it.

His body was hard, hot, alive with a furious need that was more exciting than anything Hannah had ever known. Wrapping her legs around his taut hips, she moved with him, fueling Trace's passion as she renewed her own.

Their bodies were as one. Fire sparked where their flesh joined, passion flowed between their parted lips. Heart pounding against heart, release ultimately came in a shimmering glow of enchantment.

REALITY RETURNED SLOWLY, gently. Hannah was lying in Trace's arms, her hair fanned out across his chest, her fingers playing idly in the soft curls beneath her cheek. Her skin was flushed, her body felt absolutely boneless and her mind was floating on gilded clouds of pleasure. She felt wonderful.

"You, lady, are something else," he murmured, caressing her from her creamy shoulder to her hip.

Hannah was amazed that even now, even after all they'd shared, his slow, tantalizing caress could create such an instant flare of hunger. Having never experienced such decadent physical needs, she wondered if a year and a half of celibacy had succeeded in turning her into a nymphomaniac.

Trace saw the warm sensuality in her eyes and thanked whatever gods or fates had brought Hannah Greene to New Chance. He laughed, feeling incredibly pleased with himself, with his sexy, adorable Hannah, with life.

"You're beautiful." He framed her face in his hands. "You smell like wildflowers under a bright yellow sun. And your skin is as soft as the first pussy willows in springtime." His hands caressed her breasts. "And you taste absolutely incredible."

When his tongue flicked at her rosy nipples, Hannah felt a slow, insistent tug between her legs that was every bit as wanton as it was wonderful. A nymphomaniac, she decided wonderingly. At her age. Who ever would have thought it possible?

"You're something else yourself, Sheriff," she said, slipping out of his light embrace.

"Think so?"

Hannah rose to her knees. The smile she gave him was devilishly wicked. "You're beautiful."

"Men aren't beautiful."

"Some men are," she argued, gazing possessively down at his supine body. "And you're definitely the most beautiful of the lot."

"Seen a lot of naked men, have you?" Trace had to grit his teeth as her hands traced the contours of his body, lingering devastatingly close to that part of him that had begun to respond to her tantalizing caresses.

"Enough. Janet—she was my best friend—bought me one of those sexy-buns calendars for my birthday last year."

"You're kidding." The thought of Hannah Greene ogling Mr. January's bare butt was strangely disconcerting.

Hannah laughed at Trace's offended male pride. "Don't worry," she soothed, "you'd be my choice for any month."

"That's reassuring," Trace said grumpily, wondering what Hannah had done to his mind. Was he actually jealous of twelve anonymous guys she'd never even met? Twelve naked hunks, he reminded himself. And the answer was a resounding yes.

Hannah heard the unmistakable jealousy in Trace's deep voice and was thrilled. Bending down, she brushed her lips against his frowning mouth.

"Have I told you that I absolutely adore the way you taste?" she asked silkily. Her hair formed a dark curtain in front of her face and skimmed his body as her tongue gathered in miniscule, crystal beads of salt from his chest. "Your skin is so wonderfully tangy." Her lips trailed over his rib cage. "And dark." Her breath feathered the hair on his thighs. "Mysterious."

There was certainly nothing mysterious about the bold erection jutting upward from its nest of crisp ebony hair. Knowing that she could create such a response gave Hannah a heady feeling of power. One that she was determined to test further.

Ignoring Trace's ragged protestations, she continued kissing him—his chest, his hips, his legs, his feet. When she took him between her lips in the most intimate kiss of all, Trace experienced a surge of something stronger than passion, more lasting than desire. Then, unable to hold back another moment, he lifted her up and lowered her onto him. Wonder washed over her in warm, churning waves, and she remained still, soaking it in. Then she began to move in a rhythm as old as time, driving them to the very brink of reason. And beyond.

SHE WAS LIKE NO ONE he'd ever known. She'd given herself to him tonight, openly, eagerly. And whether she was ready to admit it or not, she was his, all his.

Trace's fingers played idly with the strands of dark hair that felt like silk against his skin. His body was sated—for the time being—but his mind was not. Making love to Hannah had only confirmed what he'd suspected for days—he loved her. Never having been one to censor his thoughts, he wanted, more than anything else, to shout his love from the rooftops.

The only problem with that, he considered as he brushed the hair away from her forehead and pressed a light kiss against her temple, was that he didn't think Hannah was ready for a sudden declaration of love. She'd explained, and he reluctantly understood, that she had a great deal on her mind, trying to open the Red Rock on time and under budget. He'd just have to wait until Christmas, Trace decided regretfully.

Still, there was a lot to be said for a New Year's Eve wedding . . .

Having latched on to that happy thought, Trace wrapped both arms around her and drifted off into a satisfied, peaceful sleep.

SHE WAS FLOATING in that misty morning realm that lay somewhere between sleep and awakening. Her body ached with a vague but pleasant discomfort that brought back erotic memories. Memories that had the power to excite her, even now. Snuggling deeper into her pillow, she rolled over and reached for Trace. Hannah's lazy feeling of pleasure disintegrated the moment she encountered empty space.

After all they'd shared—the tender caresses, the whispered endearments, the total intimacy—she was suddenly afraid that Trace was no different from so many other men. How could she have misjudged him? She moaned, rolling over onto her back and pulling the sheet over her head.

She answered her own question—it was sex, pure and simple. She'd been attracted to Trace from the beginning. And why not? He was a handsome, vital, sexually compelling man. And she'd been alone, deprived of a man's touch, a man's love for so long. It wasn't at all surprising that given enough time in Trace's company she'd end up in bed with him. So why was she feeling so let down? She certainly wasn't the first woman in the world to experience a night of hedonistic pleasure and Hannah was certain she wouldn't be the last.

As long as she kept things in their proper perspective, as long as she remembered that what she and Trace Mur-

phy had shared had been highly enjoyable recreational sex
and nothing more, everything would be all right.

Hannah had nearly managed to convince herself of that
when Trace walked in the door, carrying a breakfast tray
and looking like every woman's secret fantasy.

"Damn," he said by way of greeting, "I was hoping to
get back before you woke up."

"I thought you'd gone back to your own room." Hannah cringed when she heard the unmistakable grievance
in her voice.

"I called room service, but since we neglected to put out
our order last night before going to bed, they said it'd be
forty-five minutes before they could deliver a cup of coffee. So, in order to keep you from discovering my deep,
dark secret, I decided I'd better go down and fetch it myself."

"Secret?"

He grinned. "That I'm useless in the morning until my
second cup of coffee."

His gilded chestnut hair was tousled, as if he'd combed
it by running his fingers through it. He was wearing a black
shirt that for some indiscernible reason made her think of
a pirate, and a pair of low-slung jeans that hugged his hips
in a way that made her fingers itch to touch him once
again. The boots he wore seemed to contribute to the dis-
tinctly male swagger in his walk.

Or perhaps it was memories of last night that had him
swaggering, she considered, remembering how in the heat
of passion Trace had insisted that she admit to being his.
All his. Something she'd been more than willing to do at
the time.

Hannah suffered a momentary qualm that in the bright
light of day, Trace might choose to misinterpret her words,
but then she looked into his eyes and her dread of giving

up even a smidgen of control to this man was immediately overwhelmed by another amazing jolt of desire.

It was sex, she assured herself as she felt herself melting into the sheets. Chemistry. Nothing more. But then Trace smiled at her—a smile gilded with intimate promise and sensual memories—and Hannah wondered.

"I also brought some muffins," he said, his emerald gaze not moving from her face. "The waitress assured me that they're made with fresh blueberries."

"I like blueberry muffins."

"I was hoping you would. But just in case, I also got a couple of croissants. With cheese filling."

His green eyes were turning dark and dangerous, the color of a wild, storm-tossed sea. Hannah felt her pulse quicken. "Sounds like a veritable feast."

"I'm glad you approve."

Her lips were dark pink, and slightly swollen from having been kissed again and again during the love-filled night. Remembering their taste in vivid detail, Trace felt his body tighten and was glad he was still holding the tray in front of him. No point in letting Hannah know he was rapidly turning into a sex maniac. The one thing he didn't want to do was scare her away.

A nymphomaniac, Hannah confirmed as something dark and insistent curled outward from her most feminine core. She was becoming obsessed with sex. "Oh, I approve, Sheriff," she said, her gaze offering him an unmistakably sensual invitation. "Of everything you do."

Trace approached the bed and stared down at her. He'd lost the ability to control his mind, his body, his heart. "Exactly how hungry are you?"

"Do you have to ask?"

Her warm smile caused a surge of pleasure through his body that was so intense it was almost painful. Trace put the tray down on a nearby dresser and returned to sit on the edge of the bed.

"What is it about you?" he murmured wonderingly as his fingers skimmed over her upturned face. "Why can't I get you out of my mind?" His lips followed the path warmed by his fingertips. "How is it that you smile at me and I ache? You touch and I burn."

"It's the same for me," she whispered breathlessly. As if to prove her words, Hannah linked her fingers together behind his neck and urged him down to her.

Needing no second invitation, Trace went willingly.

"You were wrong."

Trace was stretched out on the bed, busy spreading butter onto his muffin. At her sudden pronouncement, he looked up at her curiously. "About what?"

"About your being useless before your second cup of coffee."

He grinned. "It wasn't bad, was it?"

"It was—" Hannah stopped, searching for the right word. "—magnificent," she decided, her cheeks flushing at the recent memory. "You were magnificent."

Trace decided he loved the soft color that drifted into Hannah's delicate cheeks. She reminded him of an innocent schoolgirl. Not that there was anything bashful about her in bed. He'd suspected all along that a warm, passionate woman lurked beneath that workaholic exterior, but Hannah had topped even his wildest expectations.

"Hey, although I'd never turn down a compliment concerning my lovemaking techniques, I feel obliged to point out that I didn't exactly do it myself."

The rosy hue in her cheeks darkened to crimson. Lowering her gaze, Hannah turned her attention to refilling their cups.

Trace reached out, covering her hand with his. "The credit doesn't go to me alone, Hannah," he said quietly. "Or to you, as delectable and desirable as you are. It's us. And what we are together."

The conversation was suddenly becoming uncomfortable. Hannah slipped her hand from his and began brushing croissant crumbs from the rumpled sheets. "As much as I hate to return to the real world," she said briskly, reminding him of Hannah Greene, the efficient, hard-driving businesswoman, "when are we starting back?"

Trace shrugged. "Checkout is at one. I figured we'd have a leisurely breakfast in bed. Then, since you've never been to Phoenix, I thought we might do little sightseeing, maybe some Christmas shopping. They've got some great toy stores in the city filled with stuff Scott'd go bonkers over. Then we could have lunch at one of the resorts and drive back late in the afternoon or early evening. How does that sound?"

How did it sound? Wonderful. And too enticing for her own good. Because as much as she wanted to deny it, Hannah knew that something was happening between her and Trace. Something that went beyond great sex. Their lovemaking this morning had been every bit as heated and passionate as last night, but it had also taken on some new dimensions. Like fun. And affection. And it was those unexpected feelings she found threatening.

"It sounds very nice. But I'm afraid I'm going to have to take a rain check."

A temper he'd been unaware of possessing flared. With effort, Trace forced it down. "May I ask why?" he inquired, matching her cool, polite tone.

She'd made him angry. Hannah stifled her sigh, assuring herself that it was better for everyone concerned to get things over with now. Before they got out of hand. Because the longer she allowed this relationship to continue, the easier it would be for all of them—Trace, herself, even Scott—to be hurt when it eventually came to an end.

"I have a great deal of work to do."

"The wiring's done, the walls are painted, the wood floor has been buffed and sealed, Jake finished the fireplace last week and there's not a pipe in the joint that leaks. Mitzi's decorator friend is supposed to be bringing the recovered chairs tomorrow, and Dad should be finishing with the cabinets as we speak. So what's left to do?"

"There are paintings to buy, dishes to wash—"

Trace waved away her words with a careless flick of the wrist. "I'll take care of the paintings."

"You?"

"Yes, me. How'd you like a couple of Brett Kendall originals?"

Brett Kendall was a Southwestern painter who'd hit the big time when interior decorators discovered Santa Fe style. Hannah had attended one of Kendall's showings at a gallery in Manhattan. His landscape paintings had been exceptional; the prices had been astronomical.

"You know my budget. I could never afford a Kendall original. In fact, I doubt if I could afford a reproduction."

"What if I told you he was willing to donate a painting? And let you hang a few others on the walls until they sold?"

"You're kidding."

"Nope."

"Why would Brett Kendall give a painting to a woman he doesn't even know?"

"Simple. I vouched for you."

Hannah's eyes narrowed. "How do you know Brett Kendall?"

"Brett lives in New Chance. He and I grew up together."

"Thank you," she said quietly. "Although you shouldn't have bothered. You've already done so much."

"Brett's looking forward to having a spot in town to display his work," Trace said simply. "So, that's one little problem out of the way. Now, as for the dishes, I thought I saw a commercial dishwasher being delivered day before yesterday."

"You did. But it doesn't load itself."

"You're not due to open for two and a half more weeks," Trace pointed out. "Don't tell me it takes that long to load a damn dishwasher."

"Of course not."

"So? I still don't see where the place will collapse if you take a few hours to enjoy yourself." His brows grew together as he gave her a long, accusing look. "Or is it that you can't stand the idea of spending the day alone with me?"

"That's not it at all."

Trace reminded himself, not for the first time since meeting Hannah, that he'd never enjoyed things that came too easily. There was, however, a limit to even his patience. Biting back the retort that came immediately to mind, he cupped her downcast chin in his fingers, forcing her guilty gaze to his.

"Let me give you a piece of professional advice, sweetheart." His eyes had turned to ice.

"What?"

"You should never lie. Especially to a cop."

Hannah's mouth went dry; she swallowed. "What makes you think I'm lying?"

His smile did not reach his hard green eyes. "Let's just call it professional instinct. And the fact that you're a lousy liar."

Hannah did not argue; there was no need. "I really would like to spend the day with you, Trace."

"So what's the problem?" he asked, genuinely confused.

Trace knew Hannah had not been feigning the passion she'd demonstrated all night. Nor had she pretended the carefree pleasure they'd shared this morning. So why was she afraid of a simple thing like spending the day together? It wasn't as if he'd planned to drag her to the floor of F.A.O. Schwarz and have his way with her or anything.

He made it sound so simple. "It's difficult to explain," Hannah said haltingly.

"Try."

His expression was hard, implacable, giving her an idea of what he must have looked like when facing down that bank robber who'd taken the three hostages. The look only served to remind her that Trace was a cop. A universal symbol of authority who would undoubtedly insist on the same blind obedience at home as he received on the job.

For nineteen long and often terrifying months, Hannah had struggled to achieve a sense of her own identity. As much as she loved the way Trace made her feel, she couldn't—wouldn't—permit him to take over her life.

She was trying to find the words to explain her feelings when the harsh ringing of the telephone shattered the uncomfortable silence. Muttering a curse, Trace reached for it. Her nails digging moon-shaped gouges into her palms, Hannah watched. And waited.

"You're off the hook," he said gruffly as he returned the receiver to the cradle with more force than was necessary. "I've got to get back."

"Jake again," she said, knowing the answer ahead of time.

His nod was brusque, dismissing. He left the bed. "He took a potshot at Mel Skinner this morning. Not surprisingly, Mel's pressing charges of attempted murder."

"Jake tried to kill someone?" Hannah could not imagine Jake, even drunk, stooping to such violent behavior.

"Hell, if he wanted to kill the guy, he wouldn't have missed," Trace muttered, confirming Hannah's own thoughts. "Jake's a crack shot. The problem is that, intent aside, he can't go around shooting at people. He's got to learn that the days of the Wild West are dead and gone and New Chance isn't Dodge City."

"What's going to happen to him?"

"He's going to have to stay in jail until his case comes to trial."

"You don't think he'll get out on bail?"

"Given his recent behavior, would you let him out, if you were the presiding judge?"

"No," she answered, shaking her head sadly. "I suppose I couldn't take the chance."

"One good thing," he decided as he scooped his clothes up from the nearby chair and began putting them on.

"What's that?"

"He'll still be safely locked up December twenty-third."

"The day the government auctions off his land," Hannah said.

"Unless something happens to stop them," Trace confirmed.

"Do you think that's a possibility?"

The mattress sagged as Trace sat back down on the bed to pull on his boots. "No. I'm afraid I don't."

They shared a long, bleak look. Jake's very real problems made their own personal dilemmas seem trivial by comparison.

"Trace?" Hannah said softly.

The regret in her soft eyes echoed his own. Unable to resist her tender appeal, he reached out and twisted a strand of ebony hair around his finger. "I know."

Relieved that he seemed to understand, she let out a long, shuddering breath. "It's just that it's so difficult."

No, Trace corrected silently. *It's that you make it difficult.* "Let's just take things one day at a time," he suggested, but what he really wanted to do was go down to the Jeep, retrieve his handcuffs from the glove compartment and chain her to the brass headboard until she agreed to spend the rest of her life with him.

Relief and gratitude flooded into her eyes, telling Trace that although it definitely wasn't his first choice, he'd said the right thing.

"One day at a time," she agreed.

As she surrendered to the glory of his kiss, Hannah refused to permit herself to think about tomorrow.

10

To Hannah's vast relief, work on the Red Rock, as well as her relationship with Trace, went more smoothly than she could have hoped for. Unless some major, unforeseen catastrophe occurred, the restaurant would open in time for Christmas, as scheduled. Meanwhile Trace continued working nights at the café, after which they'd return to her house to make love, but he seemed to have accepted the rules adopted in Phoenix.

One day at a time. Sticking to that agreement, their relationship remained unthreatening, satisfying and practical. So why, Hannah wondered, as she watched him drive away in the pre-dawn hours, did she suddenly feel like weeping?

One week after Trace's award dinner, Hannah was awakened by Scott leaping onto her bed. "Hey, Mom, guess what?"

"Mmmph." Hannah rolled over, burrowing her face into her pillow. It was Sunday, the one morning she allowed herself to sleep in until eight o'clock before heading down to the café.

Scott was not easily deterred. "It snowed last night."

"Good for it." She smelled coffee and decided she was still dreaming.

"I kinda thought it might be fun to go sledding."

She squeezed her eyes tightly shut, fighting against the rising awareness. "We don't have a sled."

"Sure we do. Trace brought one over. He says he knows this really neat hill where he used to go sledding when he was a kid."

"I still do," offered an unmistakable voice.

That, along with the now pervasive aroma of coffee, did it. Hannah's eyes flew open and she sat up just as Trace walked into her bedroom.

"What are you doing here?"

Trace lifted a teasing brow as she clutched the blanket to her chest. He remembered a time, only a few hours ago, when she'd been a great deal less modest. "Bringing you your morning coffee."

A sled, she recalled. Scott had said something about a sled. "You came all the way over here to make coffee?"

Trace decided that this was not the time to point out that if Hannah had allowed him to spend the night, as he'd wanted to, he wouldn't have had to leave in a blinding snowstorm at five this morning, only to return three hours later.

"It's only three blocks," he reminded her, handing her the handcrafted earthenware mug. "And I wanted to bring Scott the sled."

"Well, that was certainly thoughtful of you," she admitted, blowing on the coffee to cool it. She turned her attention to her son, who looked about ready to explode with anticipation. "Did you thank Trace?"

"Sure. Well, can we?"

"Can we what?"

"Go sledding."

The coffee was rich, strong and every bit as good as any she would have made. For some strange reason the thought of Trace taking over her kitchen without her permission irritated her. "I have to work."

"But Mom, you should see all the snow! It's perfect for sledding. And Trace promised to show me this hill." His tone was perilously close to a whine. He was dressed in his NFL pajamas, a cowboy hat perched on his head. He'd been wearing the hat almost continuously since Trace had first given it to him, although Hannah had put her foot down when he wanted to wear it in the bathtub.

She was in no mood to argue. Especially when she could remember all too well her own youthful excitement at the first snow of the season. "All right. You can go."

"I told you she'd come across," Scott said to Trace as he flung his arms around Hannah's neck. Coffee sloshed over the edge of the mug. "You're the greatest mom in the whole world." He was gone in a flash. A moment later she heard him rummaging in his closet as he searched out his snow clothing.

Made unreasonably nervous by Trace's presence in her bedroom first thing in the morning, she took a tissue from the box on the bedside table and began dabbing ineffectually at the coffee stains on the thick down comforter.

Disappearing into the bathroom across the hall, Trace returned with a dampened hand towel. "Here, try this."

"Thank you." Still not quite meeting his gaze, Hannah took the towel and continued her efforts. "Bringing Scott that sled was a very thoughtful thing to do," she said.

Biting back his frustration, Trace stuck his hands in his pockets to keep from shaking her. Or loving her. At this moment it was a toss-up which he wanted to do more.

"You're welcome. Although you should probably hear the rest of my plans before you compliment me on my thoughtfulness."

Something in his tone captured her immediate attention. Hannah lifted a wary gaze to his face. "The rest of your plans?"

"Scott and I are going sledding, Hannah. But not alone."

Comprehension was instantaneous. "I can't go with you."

"Of course you can."

"The café—"

"Is ready to open. Face it, Hannah, there's nothing left to do." Something flashed in his eyes, something dark and dangerous. "There's no place for you to hide. Not today."

She rubbed at her temple, where a headache threatened. "I don't know."

He sat down on the bed and put his arm around her. "How long has it been since you've played in the snow, Hannah?" he asked, nuzzling her neck. "Remember sledding, snowball fights, making angels in the snow? Tell me that doesn't sound the least bit appealing and I'll leave. Right now."

Her flesh warmed where his lips touched, her heart quickened its beat as he nibbled lightly, possessively on her earlobe. Hannah closed her eyes and allowed herself to be tempted.

"Why can't I ever say no to you?" she asked, bewildered.

He trailed his lips up her cheek, watching the roses begin to bloom there. There was so much passion simmering under her smooth surface. What man could resist its potent allure? He, for one, had been held captive from the start.

"You told me no this morning," Trace reminded her. "When I wanted to stay in this bed. With you."

His fingers were stroking the base of her neck, his lips were creating exquisite sensations at her temple. Hannah felt herself succumbing, as she always did. "I didn't want to give Mrs. MacGregor any more grist for her gossip mill."

Personally, Trace didn't give a damn about Mrs. MacGregor or her gossip mill. Actually, when it came right down to it, he'd never given a damn what anyone in New Chance thought about him. Or the way he lived his life. But he knew Hannah did. And that, it seemed, made all the difference.

"I know. That's the only reason I left," he said.

Hannah leaned against his chest, finding comfort and warmth in his arms. "You were angry," she murmured.

He kissed her hair, breathing in the scent of flowers. "I didn't realize it showed."

"It did." She lifted her hand to his cheek. He'd shaved, but the feel of his morning beard against her heated flesh still lingered in her memory, creating a now familiar flood of desire. "But you came back."

"I came back." He turned his head, burying his lips in her palm.

When his teeth closed on the fleshy part of her hand, Hannah gasped, almost spilling the rest of the coffee. Taking the cup from her, Trace put it on the table. Then he gathered her into his arms, tearing at her control with a deep, draining kiss.

"Hey, Mom." At the sudden interruption, Hannah froze. Then, struggling against Trace's light hold, she tried to break away, but he wouldn't let her.

"Your mother's busy right now," he said genially over the top of her head.

"Yeah, I can see that," Scott allowed. "But this is an emergency."

Hannah pushed against his chest. "Trace . . ."

"Let me handle this," he murmured against her ear. "What kind of emergency?" he asked. "And it better be good."

Scott considered Trace's warning for a moment. "I guess it could wait," he decided. "Until you and Mom finish kissing."

Trace nodded approvingly. "That's more like it. Your Mom will meet you in the kitchen in a few minutes, ready for a day of fun and frolic in the snow."

"Okay." Scott turned in the doorway. "Could you ask her if she knows where my boots are? When you're finished with that mushy stuff?"

Trace grinned. "I'll try to remember to bring it up," he promised.

They were no sooner alone when Hannah turned on him. "You had absolutely no right to do that."

"Kiss you?"

"Take my place with *my* son."

"Don't be ridiculous...."

"Ridiculous?" Her voice rose. "You walk in unannounced and uninvited, take over my kitchen, usurp my position with my son, which you've been trying to do all along, and you call me ridiculous for objecting?"

"I'd definitely call your behavior overreacting," Trace shot back. "Not to mention paranoid."

His irritation only served to fuel her own. Throwing back the covers, she leaped from the bed, splayed her hands on her hips and glared down at him. "Next time you want to enter this house, you'd better have a search warrant, Sheriff," she retorted, tossing her head.

He unfolded his length from the bed. They were standing toe to toe. Trace's face was inches from hers and as fury rocketed through him, a storm swirled in his eyes. "You really like living dangerously, don't you, sweetheart?" he growled.

Hannah stared up at him, both frightened and fascinated at the same time. "You'd never hurt me."

Trace watched the trust slowly replace shock in Hannah's eyes. He wanted to take her in his arms and soothe away the acrimony that had sprung up between them. Not daring himself to touch her while his emotions hung by such a tattered thread, he slipped his hands into his pockets and shook his head in mute frustration.

"Talk about daring the devil," he muttered. "What makes you think that?"

Her eyes skimmed over his face, seeking reassurance. "I know you."

He'd never met anyone who ran as hot and cold as Hannah Greene. Trace shook his head at the futility of this discussion. "Do you?" he asked, more to himself than to her. "I wonder."

She wanted to go to him. Into his arms. Into his bed. Forever. Instead, Hannah lifted her hand to his chest. She could feel his heartbeat under her fingertips. Only hours before, she'd imagined she could taste the strong, wild rhythm beneath her lips.

"Perhaps we should spend the day together after all," she suggested softly. "So I can learn more about you."

He covered her hand with his, his gaze more solemn than she'd ever seen it. "You realize, don't you, Hannah, that works both ways."

The challenge was there, lingering in the air between them, waiting for her to pick it up. Linking their fingers together, Hannah brushed her lips against his knuckles. "Yes."

Trace gave a low, appreciative laugh. "Then come on, sweetheart," he said, ruffling her hair with an easy affection that told her the charged moment had passed. For now. "Before all that white stuff out there melts."

He wrapped his arms around her, drawing her to him for another one of the kisses that never ceased to take her breath away. She could feel the strong, masculine imprint of his body through her white cotton nightgown and her need soared.

"You'd better get dressed," he said after a long, luxurious pause. "Before I come up with a better way to spend a leisurely Sunday with my girl." He brushed his hands possessively over her breasts, a satisfied gleam in his eyes as he watched the nipples harden under his intimate touch. "I'll help the kid find his boots."

Hannah nodded, her own heart shining in her eyes. After Trace left, she began gathering up her warm clothing. Outside, a light snow was still falling, covering the ground in a soft, fluffy blanket of white. Suddenly feeling unbelievably lighthearted, Hannah found herself looking forward to the day ahead.

SWATHED IN SNOW, New Chance looked like an idyllic scene from a Currier and Ives print. The temperature had dropped dramatically during the night. Icicles hung like crystal ornaments from shaggy, snow-coated evergreens while lacy snowflakes danced on intermittent gusts of wind.

"I'd forgotten how much I like winter," Hannah murmured as she and Trace walked hand in hand toward the hill outside of town. Scott had run on ahead, dragging the sled behind him, accompanied by Merlin, who was happily plowing through chest-deep drifts of snow. "There's something magical about snow. It always reminds me of fairy tales and ice castles."

"Don't forget the slush and shovels," Trace said. "Not to mention road closures and chains and stranded tourists from the desert who have absolutely no idea how to drive in snow and who constantly have to be pulled out of drifts and—"

"Hey." Hannah punched him lightly on his upper arm. "It was your idea to drag me out here, so don't you dare go spoiling my fantasy with reality."

"I wouldn't think of it," he said.

Hannah smiled her approval. "That's better."

Trace looked down at her. Her cheeks were already rosy, her laughing eyes as bright as diamonds. "Speaking of fantasies." Pulling her into a grove of trees, he framed her face in his gloved hands.

"Trace." They were nearing the hill and she could hear the gleeful shouts and laughter drifting on the crisp morning air. "Someone might see us."

Trace wondered if there was anyone left in New Chance who wasn't aware of the fact that the sheriff was courting the widow Greene and decided that there probably wasn't. "Let them."

"But . . ."

"My sweet, lovely Hannah," he said patiently, "don't you think almost everyone around these parts has already figured out that I'm not spending all my spare time with you because you're in need of police protection?"

"We're friends."

"While I can always use another friend, I'd say our relationship is a great deal more intimate than that, sweetheart." As he ran his hand down her side, Trace wondered idly who the hell had invented down jackets. It definitely took a great deal of the fun out of playing in the snow. "We also happen to be lovers."

She tried to move away, only to find her escape impeded by a silver-white aspen. "Even so, there's no reason to advertise that fact," she insisted. "I especially don't like Scott seeing us together the way we were this morning."

Whenever Trace felt he was making progress, every time he thought that Hannah was beginning to allow him into her life, into her son's life, she suddenly turned around and set up new barricades. Tired of skirting his way around the artificial barriers, Trace decided to crash right through this one.

"If you're talking about me kissing his mother," he said, backing her against the trunk of the tree, "then he's just going to have to get used to it. Because I have every intention of kissing you every time those lusciously seductive lips get within puckering range."

Then, as if to prove his intentions, Trace gathered her in his arms and covered her mouth with his, kissing her with a sweet and wild passion that never ceased to thrill her. Her lips parted, her arms twined around his neck and she leaned against him, wrapped in a warm cocoon of pleasure.

The shouts and laughter of children echoed from the nearby hill. In the bare winter branches of the aspen overhead a blue jay scolded noisily. Dogs barked at fluffy-tailed squirrels who ran to the top of trees and chattered furiously back at them. The woods were alive with joyful winter sounds, but Hannah remained oblivious to everything but the glorious pressure of Trace's lips moving hungrily on hers, leading her out of the icy wonderland into a world of dazzling flames and dense smoke.

Much, much later—it could have been minutes, hours or an eternity—Trace lifted his head. "Do you have any idea how much I want to drag you into the nearest snowdrift and make love to you?"

"In a snowdrift?" Her fingers were still linked behind his neck; despite her earlier fears of being discovered, Hannah found herself in no hurry to remove them. "People keep telling me that you Murphys are crazy. Perhaps they're right."

"Perhaps." His smiling lips skimmed up her cheek, leaving sparks wherever they touched. "This Murphy's definitely crazy about you."

"Still, wouldn't a snowdrift be a little chilly?"

"A bed, then. A soft bed with thick, fluffy comforters and satin sheets."

How was it that he could beguile her with a mere look, an innocent touch, and the lush velvet of his voice? Hannah held on to Trace's shoulders as the ground began to slip slowly out from under her.

"I've heard satin sheets are slippery."

"Spoilsport." His roving mouth returned to hers. "That's okay, I've got a better idea, anyway."

"Oh?" The thermometer on the side of her house had declared the temperature to be a brisk thirty-six degrees, but Hannah knew her own temperature was rapidly reaching the boiling point.

"On a fur rug, in front of a blazing fire, your ivory skin gleaming in the dancing light from the flames."

Hannah looked up into his eyes, which blazed like dark emeralds, and felt herself melting. "I don't have a fireplace."

"No problem, I do. Remember?"

"Ah, but you don't have a fur rug."

"It just so happens that Mitzi gave me a fake tiger stadium blanket for my last birthday. Will that do?"

Hannah tilted her head as she appeared to consider that for a moment. "I suppose, if we both used our imaginations, it might suffice."

Trace's eyes held hers for several long, pulsating seconds. "Tonight."

Her exhaled breath formed a frosty ghost between them. "Tonight," she agreed.

Tonight. Only twelve, thirteen long hours away. As he took her hand in his and began walking toward the hill again, Trace wondered how he was going to wait.

MONDAY MORNING. Hannah had overslept, the toaster seemed to only have two shades—black and blacker— she'd forgotten to buy milk, forcing Scott to eat his Captain Crunch dry, and the heater was making strange noises that sounded as if someone or something were dying in the duct work. It was not, Hannah decided, a propitious way to begin the week.

"Are you going to marry Trace?"

The question came from out of the blue as Hannah was scraping the blackened toast into the sink.

"What?"

Scott reached into the brightly colored box, extracting a handful of the sugarcoated cereal Hannah usually only allowed him to eat on weekends.

"Are you going to marry Trace?"

"Of course not. Where on earth did you get an idea like that?"

"Mitzi's marrying Dan. On Christmas Eve."

Hannah had given up trying to get her son to refer to Trace's father as Mr. Murphy. Especially as Dan himself had insisted formality had no place in New Chance. "I know. And I'm very happy for them, but what does that have to do with Trace and me?"

"Trace says his dad's marrying Mitzi because they're in love." There was an obvious question in his voice.

"I'm sure that's the case." Hannah gave a pointed look at her watch. "If you don't want to be late for school, young man, you'd better get moving."

"I won't be late. Trace looks at you the same way."

The heater rattled ominously. The weather forecast had called for more snow this afternoon. Hannah said a small, silent prayer that the ancient heater wouldn't choose today, of all days, to die on her. "What way?" she asked absently, wondering what service calls cost in New Chance.

"The same way Dan looks at Mitzi," Scott explained with exaggerated patience, as if he were speaking to a particularly slow preschooler. "So, are you going to get married?"

"No, we're not," Hannah said firmly. "And if you don't hurry, I'm going to have to drive you to school, which I don't have time to do because I'm suppose to meet Brett Kendall at the Red Rock at eight-thirty."

But Scott was not to be so easily deterred. "But if Trace loves you . . ."

"If Trace loved me, which he doesn't," Hannah warned sternly, "it would be none of your business, young man. Now, if you're finished with breakfast, it's past time to gather up your jacket and boots."

Hannah gave her son her sternest look, and although he appeared inclined to argue, Scott apparently thought better of it and left the kitchen. Minutes later, he'd returned, dressed for outdoors. The ever-present cowboy hat was perched atop his red-and-blue wool cap.

"Are you mad at me?"

Hannah sighed and went down on her knees, wrapping her arm around his slender shoulders. "Me? Mad? Where did you get an idea like that?"

"Whenever I talk about you and Trace you yell at me."

"I don't yell."

"Yes, you do. It's just kinda quiet yelling," Scott insisted.

"Perhaps I do," she admitted. "And I'm sorry."

A forgiving smile bloomed on his face. "That's okay, Mom. Trace says everybody can have an off day once in a while."

Trace again. There seemed to be no avoiding the man. "I suppose he's right."

"Sure he is. And he's real nice, too, huh, Mom?"

"Real nice," she agreed softly.

"Then you really do like him? At least a little bit?"

Hannah had never believed in lying to her son and she wasn't about to begin now. "I really do like him. A lot."

"If you like him a lot, then why don't you get married?"

"Scott . . ."

"Gee, look at the time!" Breaking free of her light embrace, he grabbed his books from the table. "I gotta get going or Mrs. Patterson'll make me stay after school." He turned in the kitchen doorway. "Would you at least think about marrying Trace?"

"I've already told you. . . ."

"Just think about it, okay, Mom?"

She was late for her meeting, and Scott was nearly late for school. Deciding this was not the time to continue arguing the matter, Hannah threw her hands up in the air. "Okay, I'll think about it."

Scott's answering grin was broad and knowing. "Neat!"

He was gone in a flash, leaving her kneeling on the rag rug, not knowing whether to laugh or to cry.

TRACE SPENT the next three days in Phoenix in a final, last-ditch effort to extricate Jake Brennan from his troubles with the government. If Hannah was upset by how much she'd come to care for New Chance's sheriff, she was appalled by how much she missed him while he was gone.

The renovation on the Red Rock was finally complete.

The kitchen cabinets, thanks to Dan Murphy's oil and elbow grease, gleamed like an early-morning sunrise and the bright copper hood looked brand-new.

During the last week, people kept streaming in with gifts of time and goods. Helen Jacobson, from New Chance Mercantile, brought a selection of wicker and rattan baskets that were perfect for the lush green plants Cal Potter's wife, Lillian, had grown in her backyard greenhouse. Brett Kendall, Trace's friend and New Chance's resident artist, had donated an oil painting that portrayed the Red Rock Café looking quaint and inviting with a snow-capped Mingus Mountain looming in the background. Other artists, from nearby Sedona, not wanting to be left out, had offered paintings on consignment that Hannah gratefully accepted, and soon the Navaho-white walls were ablaze with vivid color.

To her delight, New Chance proved to be a treasure-trove of artisans. Residents arrived with bright rugs woven on homemade looms and earthenware dishes thrown on potters' wheels in home studios. Mitzi, using her contacts throughout the valley, had succeeded in getting the story of the Red Rock's revival—and the café's new owner—into the life-style sections of the *Mingus County Courier*, the *Sedona Citizen* and the *Flagstaff Daily Progress*. The flood of reservations generated by the advance publicity would have warmed the heart of the most jaded Manhattan restaurateur. Hannah had been moved to tears.

Before her disbelieving eyes, The Red Rock Café had become a dream come true. And as each day passed, she began to feel as if New Chance was where she'd always belonged, a feeling that was enhanced after an hour-long telephone conversation with Janet Morrison. Although Hannah had enjoyed talking with her friend—hearing the latest club gossip and in turn telling her all about the Red Rock's renovation—Connecticut seemed a lifetime away.

Everything was wonderful. Perfect. Except for Trace.

She sat alone in the café, drinking in the warm, inviting atmosphere as she studied the menus that had been delivered from the printer in Flagstaff. For some reason, holding the tan menu with the bold dark script in her hand made her dream seem real for the first time. Tomorrow the truck from the wholesaler would make its first delivery. And in three short days the Red Rock would open. It hardly seemed possible.

She was staring into the fire she'd built in Jake Brennan's beehive fireplace, imagining the café filled with the hum of conversation, the rattle of cutlery, the aromas of hearty food drifting out from the kitchen, when Scott suddenly burst through the door.

"Hey Mom, guess what?"

"You got an A on your math test." They'd spent several hours last night unraveling the mysteries of long division.

"Nah. Well, that too. But this is something a lot better."

Hannah looked over at her son; he seemed about to burst. "I give up."

"We're going to go chop down a Christmas tree! Me and Trace. And you, too," he tacked on as an afterthought.

"Trace and I." So he was back. Hannah felt her heartbeat quicken and wondered what it was about the man that made her behave like a besotted teenager.

"Yeah. All three of us," Scott agreed impatiently. "Trace says he knows a neat place where the fattest, tallest trees grow."

Hannah glanced outside. A light snow was falling, making the crackling fire seem even more inviting. "I thought we'd buy a tree, like we do every year."

"In this part of the country, buying a tree when you can cut it yourself is viewed as heresy." Trace said as he entered the restaurant, stamping snow off his boots.

Hannah couldn't stop the smile from blooming on her face. He'd been gone three days. Seventy-two hours. It had seemed like a lifetime. She was suddenly so very tired. Tired of trying to keep Trace out of her thoughts, out of her life. She rose from the table.

"It sounds wonderful. Just give me five minutes to pack us a lunch and I'll be ready."

He'd expected an argument. All the way back from Phoenix, he'd tried to think up an answer for every pale excuse Hannah might offer. That she acquiesced so quickly gave him hope that the rest of the day—and his carefully planned evening—would go just as well.

His gaze was locked onto her face—that luminous face he hadn't been able to get out of his mind during those long and lonely nights in Phoenix. "Hey, Scott," he said, not taking his eyes from Hannah's, "how about going out to the Jeep and keeping Merlin company while I help your mother fix lunch."

Scott's answer proved that although he might be only eight years old, he was far from blind. "You're gonna kiss her, huh?"

"We're only going into the kitchen to make sandwiches," Hannah answered quickly.

"But first I'm going to kiss your mother hello," Trace corrected. "You see, sport, I've missed your mom while I was gone. Missed her a lot."

"Mom missed you, too," Scott offered, ignoring Hannah's warning look.

"Really?"

Hannah turned toward her son. "Scott . . ."

"Really," he insisted. "She yelled at me when I tracked mud into the house. And she was grumpy a lot, and when I got up to go to the bathroom one night, she was watching television and crying. At three in the morning," he said significantly as he left the café.

Things were getting better and better, Trace decided as he walked toward Hannah. "Crying?" he asked with a lifted brow.

"I always cry when I watch *Now, Voyager*," she insisted.

"I'll accept that. The question is, what were you doing watching old movies in the wee hours of the morning?" he asked as he continued moving toward her.

"I didn't have anything else to do."

"Ever try sleeping?"

"I couldn't." This time it was Hannah who moved closer. "You weren't there."

Desire pounded in his head, echoed through his body. He gathered her in his arms and buried his lips in her hair. "Three days," he murmured. "But it seemed like forever."

Hannah sighed as she pressed her cheek against his chest. Had she ever known such contentment? It flowed over her, warm and soothing, even as excitement stirred.

When she looked up at him, her emotions, no longer guarded, were in her eyes, on her smiling lips, in the trembling of her hands as she held his face between her palms. "Forever," she agreed softly. "We'll have to make up for lost time."

Trace ran his hands down her back, around her waist, over her hips as he pulled her even closer. "Lady, that's the best offer I've had all day." He kissed her then, because it had been too long. The kiss was intoxicating, filled with sweet, sensual promise. "Tonight."

His breath was like a warm summer breeze against her lips. It was almost as if his mouth had become part of her own. "Yes," she whispered.

"I want to love you, Hannah. All night long."

She clung to him, opening her mouth to his seductive pressure. At this moment, she knew she could deny him nothing. "Yes."

"Until morning."

Hannah's need, after three long and desolate days, overrode her fear of gossip. "Until morning."

Well, it wasn't forever, Trace mused as he deepened the kiss. But it was enough. For now. Besides, if everything went as planned, by tomorrow morning Hannah would be his. For as long as they lived.

"I STILL CAN'T BELIEVE I hiked all over Mingus Mountain just for a Christmas tree," Hannah complained several hours later.

"Not just a Christmas tree," Trace corrected with a grin. "The best Christmas tree in the county."

"It's the best Christmas tree in the whole state," Scott put in. "The whole country. Probably the best in the whole entire world!"

"I wouldn't doubt it for a minute," Trace said.

"Well, all I know is that my feet turned blue hours ago, my nose is a block of ice and I can't even feel my ears."

Trace looked over at her as they pulled up in front of her house. "I didn't realize you were that uncomfortable. You should have said something, and we would have come home a long time ago."

The gentle concern in his gaze threatened to be her undoing. That he cared about her a great deal was obvious. It was also dangerous for a woman trying to learn to stand on her own two feet.

"It's not that bad. I was overreacting."

"You'll probably feel better after a hot bath," he suggested.

"With bubbles," Scott said. "Mom likes bubble baths," he advised Trace.

"I know." Trace's green eyes were filled with wicked humor. It hadn't been that long ago that he and Hannah had shared a most delightful bubble bath. Later, when he showed up at the office smelling like wildflowers, he'd taken a little ribbing from Cal, but it had definitely been worth it.

Hannah felt the color rising in her chapped cheeks at the memory. "A bath would be nice."

"Maybe you can wash her back, Trace," Scott said helpfully. "Dad used to do that sometimes. It made her real happy."

A small pool of silence settled over them. Hannah, fearing that Trace would resent the mention of David, pretended a sudden interest in a pair of neighborhood children's energetic effort to build a snowman.

"I'd like to make your mother happy," Trace said. He kept his tone light, but Hannah could hear the promise nevertheless.

She turned back toward him, her dark eyes glowing with emotion. "You do," she said softly.

Scott's gaze went from Hannah to Trace than back again. "Come on, Merlin," he said, tugging at the dalmatian's collar with one hand and opening the back door of the Jeep with the other, "let's go help Warren and Jackie with that snowman."

"We'll be having dinner soon," Hannah warned.

Scott looked momentarily surprised. "But . . ."

"How about making it home by five-thirty," Trace suggested, breaking in smoothly. "That'll give you half an hour to finish up Frosty." He glanced over at Hannah. "Is that okay?"

For just an instant Hannah thought she detected something pass between Trace and Scott. Something that seemed strangely like a secret shared. Then, deciding she'd imagined it, she nodded. "Five-thirty," she confirmed.

HEAVEN. Hannah leaned back, luxuriating in the frothy suds, sipping on the Amaretto-laced coffee Trace had prepared. The warm water soaked the chill out of her bones and the coffee spread a soothing warmth throughout her body, while Trace's admiring gaze, as he leaned against the sink and watched her, created a slow, simmering heat all its own. A trio of jasmine-scented candles added a tropical fragrance to the air that belied the snow falling outside.

"How did it really go in Phoenix?" Hannah asked. Although she'd asked earlier, Trace had merely responded that things might not be as bad as they seemed.

"It's looking up."

"I'm so glad." Putting her cup on the floor, Hannah picked up the bath sponge and began soaping her arms.

Trace kneeled down beside the tub, took the sponge and ran it tantalizingly up her arm. "I finally found this woman, Karen Fairfield, in accounting, who's willing to dig a bit deeper into Jake's records."

"Do you think she'll be able to locate his missing payments?" As his slow touch warmed her blood, Hannah found it difficult to keep her mind on their conversation.

"I sure hope so." He squeezed the sponge and rivulets of warm, fragrant water ran over her breasts. "Have I happened to mention that I love you?" he asked with exaggerated casualness.

Trace's quiet declaration should not have come as a surprise. Later Hannah would tell herself that she'd been expecting it for days. Weeks. At the moment, coming as it did out of a clear blue sky, it stunned her. She drew in a deep breath.

"Trace..."

"No." Abandoning the bath sponge, he pressed his fingers against her frowning lips. "It doesn't require an answer, Hannah. Not now, anyway. I just wanted you to know." He leaned forward and caressed the side of her face with his fingertips. "After all, we've got all night."

He'd only touched her cheek and her heart was pounding. "All night," she whispered, drowning in the jade depths of his warming gaze.

The sound of the screen door banging captured their unwilling attention. "I'd better get out there," Trace said without enthusiasm.

Hannah nodded. "I think it'd be best."

"I could always tell him I was washing your back."

"I'm sorry about that." Her eyes mirrored the regret in her voice.

"Hey, I've already told you that I have no problem with your having been married, Hannah. And since I hate the thought of you being unhappy, I'm glad your husband loved you. And that you loved him." He grinned as they heard Scott banging around in the kitchen. "You're just going to have to get it through that hard head of yours, Mrs. Greene, that I'm crazy about you. And I'm also crazy about that kid you and David made together."

With that he gave her a swift, brief kiss, then left the bathroom.

Unabashedly eavesdropping, Hannah heard Scott talking a mile a minute, something about Merlin and a snowball fight. When her son and Trace shared a robust laugh, some small dark spot deep inside her heart contracted. Pressing her hand against her chest, Hannah wondered how something as wonderful as love could be so painful.

11

"YOU'RE JUST IN TIME," Trace announced as Hannah entered the kitchen a few minutes later.

"In time for what?"

"Scott and I thought we'd take you out to dinner."

After spending the greater part of the day trudging through knee-deep snow on the forested slopes of Mingus Mountain, the idea of going back outside and driving to Sedona, or even nearby Cottonwood for dinner, was less than appealing.

"Thanks guys," she said, "but I was planning on fixing something simple here. How does spaghetti carbonara sound?"

Trace and Scott exchanged a brief look. Perhaps it was only her imagination, but Hannah thought her son's expression revealed momentary panic. Trace's expression was, as usual, calmly reassuring.

"It sounds great," Trace said, "but you'll have to save it for another time. Tonight's our treat."

Hannah didn't know whether it was Trace's quiet insistence, or the fact that Scott seemed to be holding his breath, or merely that she was too tired to argue. Whatever, within minutes she found herself bundled into the front seat of the Jeep, headed down Oak Street, in the opposite direction from the interstate that would take them to any of several nearby towns.

"Where are we going?"

"You'll see," Trace said.

"It's a surprise," Scott added.

She was about to delve into this new mystery when Trace pulled up in front of the Red Rock. "What are we doing here?"

"I forgot something the other day," he said, cutting the ignition.

"What?"

Trace ignored her question. "It may take me a few minutes to find it. Why don't you and Scott come in so you won't freeze sitting out here."

The snowstorm had picked up; gusts of wind were blowing thick flakes against the windshield. Hannah was not at all eager to leave the warmth of the Jeep. "That's okay. You can leave the heater on."

"Sorry, I'm afraid I can't do that."

"Why not?"

"I'm almost out of gas."

"You were going to drive to dinner with an almost empty gas tank? In this storm?" That was not at all like Trace. One of his attributes—as well as one of the things she found most irritating about him—was that he was always prepared for anything. Once she'd even accused him of being born with a Boy Scout knife clutched in his fist.

"Come on, Mom," Scott complained. "We're wasting time."

"All right." Hannah's frustrated sigh feathered her bangs. "But if I catch pneumonia going out in this storm, you two are going to have to open the Red Rock by yourselves."

"It's a deal," Trace said.

"Trace could make chili dogs," Scott decided. "And I know how to cook frozen waffles in the microwave."

"Chili dogs and waffles. What a splendid Christmas menu," Hannah said dryly as she climbed down from the passenger seat. "I wonder why I didn't think of it."

As she walked up to the small building, Hannah experienced the now familiar pride she felt every time she saw the café. It was really, truly hers. And she'd done it all by herself. Well, not really by herself; everyone in town had helped out. But she'd been the driving force behind the renovation; she was the one who was now responsible for making a success of the restaurant, something she no longer had any doubts about doing.

In the beginning, faced with David's debts, she'd acted on instinct, doing whatever was necessary to pay their many creditors. But the Red Rock was something she'd planned, something she'd worked hard for, something she'd accomplished. The run-down restaurant in a small town in north-central Arizona had given her a great deal more than a new chance; it had given her self-confidence. For the first time in her life, she felt invincible.

"Something funny?" Trace asked as she unlocked the front door.

Hannah looked up at him blankly. "Funny?"

"You were smiling."

"Was I?"

"Yep."

"You were, Mom," Scott said. "I saw you."

The smile she was now aware of widened. "I was just thinking that I felt a little bit like Superman."

"You can't be Superman," Scott argued. "You're a girl. But you could be Supergirl. Or Wonder Woman," he added magnanimously.

"I think that just for tonight, your Mom can be anything she wants to be, Scott," Trace corrected gently. "Including Superman."

Hannah inclined her head as she opened the door. "Thank you, Trace."

"Don't mention it." As he followed her into the darkened restaurant, he leaned down and murmured in her ear. "So long as you're not planning to be faster than a speeding bullet. I'd kind of planned on a long, leisurely night together."

Hannah laughed, the sadness she'd felt earlier dispelled.

It was a night she'd remember for the rest of her life. The moment she turned on the lights, the Red Rock came to life with cheering people. As her stunned eyes swept the room, Hannah guessed that everyone in town was present. Mitzi and Dan were there, of course. Grizzled Johnny Mott, the Red Rock's previous owner, was walking around, shaking his head in amazement, astounded by the transformation of the restaurant he'd owned for so many years. Cal Potter and his brother Hal had shown up, along with Fred Wiley and Mrs. MacGregor and Brett Kendall and Hank Young. Even Jake Brennan was there; Hannah discovered he had been let out on temporary parole for the evening.

The restaurant was filled to its wide oak rafters with colorful crepe-paper streamers and bright helium balloons. A foil Good Luck banner hung over the hand-carved bar Mitzi had located in a Sedona antique shop, and the array of colorful bouquets gracing the tables made it appear as if spring had come early to New Chance.

Hannah sank into a chair, staring blindly at a deceptively casual arrangement of tulips. The bright flowers blurred into a yellow-and-lavender haze as tears welled over in her eyes and began to spill down her cheeks.

"I never imagined," she murmured. "All the time, you all were planning this and I never knew."

"Speech!" Cal Potter shouted out over the laughter and the cheers. The idea spread, until everyone in the room—including Scott, Hannah noticed—was calling for her to speak. When Trace put his hands on her waist and lifted her up onto the bar, an expectant hush immediately fell over the room.

Taking a deep breath, Hannah scrubbed at her free-falling tears with the back of her hand. For some reason she could not discern, the action brought another long round of cheers. She looked down at Trace for encouragement, receiving it in the form of a slow, reassuring wink.

"Six weeks ago," she began in a voice she wished were steadier, "my son and I arrived in New Chance. We were strangers, far away from home, and although I can't speak for Scott, I'll admit now that I was scared to death. Especially when I found out that my long-awaited dream had nearly gone up in smoke."

An understanding murmur swept through the crowd. As Hannah looked down into the faces of these strangers who had become her friends, she felt her nervousness slip away.

"But some of you—Dan, Cal, Fred and Trace—" her gaze turned fond as it settled on each man in turn, lingering imperceptibly longer on Trace "—assured me that New Chance was a special place. A place where people cared about one another. Where western hospitality was not a cliché." Hannah smiled. "During these last six weeks I've discovered that you were telling the truth."

A new cheer arose as the group applauded themselves. The warmth in the room was palpable, and Hannah could feel the tears brimming over again. "New Chance is special because its people are special," she said. "And I thank you all for allowing Scott and me to become part of your lives."

This time the cheers were deafening, lasting long after Trace had helped Hannah down from the bar. He hadn't lied about taking her out to dinner; in the best tradition of a small-town potluck, everyone had brought a dish to contribute to the celebratory meal.

"HAPPY?" Trace asked later that evening as they danced to the music of the New Chance Volunteer Fire Department's country and western band.

The band, while enthusiastic, had a limited repertoire; they appeared to only know four tunes. They got around that small problem by playing the songs again and again. Dan's guitar broke its G string on a spirited rendition of *The Orange Blossom Special*, Cal Potter sang off-key and Fred Wiley's foot-tapping consistently missed the beat. Hannah thought they were wonderful.

No longer caring about what people might think about their relationship, Hannah went up on her toes and kissed Trace lightly. "This is definitely going to go down as one of the all-time best nights of my life."

Moving her hair aside, Trace brushed his lips down her neck. "The night's still young," he reminded her huskily.

As she looked up at him, Hannah's eyes filled with sensual promise. No words were spoken. None were needed.

MOONLIGHT STREAMED DOWN from a midnight-blue sky, lighting the bedroom with a radiant glow. Trace had come to know Hannah's body well; his hands moved expertly over her, warming, pleasuring, rekindling flashpoints she'd never before been aware of possessing. His hands tempted; his lips seduced. His tongue, as it breached her parted lips, promised. The fragrance of bath oil clung to her, mingling with the hot, heady scent of the night, of their love. Her skin, gleaming with a pearly luminescence in the silvery light, grew feverishly hot, arousing them both.

Unable to remain passive while he was driving her mad, Hannah's touch grew greedy. The fluffy comforter slid unnoticed onto the floor; the flower-sprigged sheets became hot and tangled. Passion built, desire flared, needs grew unmanageable.

Like a man possessed, Trace lost himself in the warm satin of her breasts, buried his mouth in the heady fragrance of her neck. When his exploring fingers dipped into her warm, welcoming moisture, raw desire tore through him, obliterating all but one thought. *More.* He wanted to take her places she'd never been, uncover secrets she'd never imagined. The past vanished; the future dimmed. There was only now. Only Hannah.

Control disintegrated as the power swept them away, into a hazy, smoldering world of their own making.

MUCH, MUCH LATER, Hannah still clung to him. She was feeling a warm and satisfied glow and would have been more than happy to stay here, wrapped in his arms, for the rest of her days. Even as common sense told her that would be a highly impractical way to spend her life, the romantic she'd discovered lurking within her could think of nothing that would bring her more pleasure.

"Damn," Trace murmured as his hands played idly in her hair.

"Well, that's certainly romantic." She pressed her lips against his chest, wondering if she'd ever tire of the taste and scent of his skin.

"Stop that," he said. Hannah could feel his deep, rough chuckle under her mouth. "How am I supposed to concentrate when you insist on seducing me?"

"Me? Seducing you?" She flicked at the dark male nub, buried in the forest of chest hair, with her tongue, rewarded when it instantly hardened.

He wound his hand through her hair, lifting her head up. "Don't play the innocent with me, woman. If we keep this up, you're going to wear out my poor, abused body before I hit thirty-six."

Hannah braced her elbow on his bare chest and cupped her chin in her palm. "I haven't heard you complaining. Until now."

Trace ran his hand down her back, loving the way he could make her tremble under his touch, even now. "It wasn't a complaint. It was just that your wild and wanton ways almost made me forget to give you your present."

"You bought me a present? Why?"

"Does there have to be a reason?"

"There usually is."

He shrugged. "Okay, I suppose we could call it a pre-grand-opening present. Or an early Christmas present. Or a just-because present."

"Just because?"

"Just because I love you."

Hearing him declare his feelings again so openly brought a soft misting of renewed tears to her eyes. "Oh, Trace..."

"Shh." He pressed a finger against her lips. "Wait until you see what it is."

Hannah watched as he left the bed and crossed the room to where his pants were draped over the arm of the wing chair. When he pulled the square velvet box from the pocket, Hannah's heart skipped a beat. Her fingers feeling like stones, Hannah slowly opened the box. The perfect pear-shaped diamond, nesting in an antique yellow-gold filigree setting, glistened like ice in the moonlight.

"Oh, Trace," Hannah whispered with a soft sigh. "It's beautiful."

"It was my grandmother's."

"I'm surprised your father didn't want to give it to Mitzi."

"Mitzi's more prone to razzle-dazzle. Flash." He was watching her carefully. "When you told me about the antiques you used to collect, I figured you preferred things with history. A past."

She ran a finger over the delicate gold weave. "I do."

"That's why I thought you might like this."

"Oh, Trace." This time her rippling sigh was filled with regret.

"I love you, Hannah. And unless I've misread everything, you love me."

"I do."

It was only a whisper, but the words he'd waited to hear reverberated in his head like a pair of brass gongs. Encouraged, Trace sat down on the edge of the bed and stroked Hannah's hair.

"Then you'll marry me?"

This time her tears were born of sadness, not pleasure. As the ring shimmered in the light, Hannah resolutely blinked them away. "I can't."

His hand froze momentarily on her shoulder. Although his touch remained gentle, there was cold, hard steel beneath. "Can't?" he asked quietly. "Or won't?"

"Does it matter?"

Trace tried to think calmly, tried to sort through this latest roadblock in order to salvage what was left of the night . . . of their lives. It wasn't easy; pride warred with love, ego with need. For the moment, pride won out.

"I see," he said tightly.

The velvet box dropped to the rumpled sheet as Hannah grasped his arms in desperation. "No, you don't," she insisted, close to panic. "You have to understand."

"That's what I'm trying to do." Although his voice remained calm, his eyes were not. "It's what I've been trying to do from the beginning."

She took a deep breath that was meant to calm, but didn't. "I don't know where to begin."

"Why don't you try at the beginning?"

His rough, sarcastic tone caused Hannah to study him warily. She'd never known him to be so abrupt, so remote. She had the horrible feeling that whatever she said, it wasn't going to make any difference. But she had to try.

"When I married David, I thought he was Prince Charming. He was my knight in shining armor."

Although such a glowing description of her former husband hurt more than he would have guessed possible, Trace was prepared to accept Hannah's feelings. "I thought we'd already established that I don't have any problems with your having been in love with your husband," he reminded her.

"We did. And I appreciate that."

"Gee, thanks."

Hannah had a fair amount of pride herself. Irritation at his derisive tone gave her a renewed strength. "Do you want to hear this or not?"

Trace would have preferred irritation. Even anger. Anything but the icy fear that was beginning to crawl over him. "Do I have any choice?" Frustrated, he rubbed his hands over his face. "Sorry," he mumbled. "Please, go on."

Emotions were etching furrows into his face. Deep lines she'd never before noticed bracketed his mouth and cut across his forehead. Hannah longed to throw herself into his arms—strong arms, she reminded herself—and spend the rest of her life, the rest of their lives, together. If it were only that simple.

"I was brought up to believe in fairy tales. In happy endings."

"There's nothing wrong with believing in happy endings," Trace felt obliged to point out. "So long as you have a contingency plan available just in case things don't work out exactly as planned."

"Don't you see?" Hannah said, dragging her hands through her hair, "that's precisely what I'm talking about. I didn't have a contingency plan. Because I left everything—every decision about my life, my son's life—to David. I was so thrilled to be married, to be his wife, that I gave up my autonomy willingly. What I didn't understand at the time was that I was totally unprepared to deal with the outside world. The real world.

"It was as if I'd spent all those years in the dark, walking toward this unseen cliff." Hannah gulped in a shuddering draught of air. "And when David died, leaving all those debts, I fell off and was left hanging from the edge by my fingertips."

"But you pulled yourself up."

"Yes. But it wasn't easy. And I'm not sure I could do it again."

"You were young when you married," Trace said.

"Nineteen."

"And David was what, thirty-five? Thirty-six?" Hannah had mentioned that her husband had been a great deal older than she, but at the time Trace hadn't grasped the significance of what she'd been trying to tell him.

"Thirty-eight."

Comprehension, when it dawned, was staggering. Suddenly he understood her continual insistence on independence, her almost obsessive drive to establish her own restaurant, the frustrating way she'd attempted to keep him at arm's length.

"Lord, Hannah, that's nearly a twenty-year difference." He could have been her father. In many ways, Trace decided, he probably had played a paternal role in Hannah's life.

"David was good for me. For the woman I was," she insisted.

"I believe that." A single tear glistened on her cheek. Trace reached out and brushed it away. "But you're not that woman any longer, Hannah. And what your David might possibly have found threatening are some of the things I love about you—your strength, your drive, even your intransigence, which at times, I'll have to admit, threatens to drive me up a wall. They're all part of who you are, who you've become. I don't want to control your life, sweetheart. I'm only asking to share it."

If that were only true. Even as Hannah felt herself succumbing to his enticing argument, she couldn't quite expunge a lingering vestige of fear.

"I want to believe you," she whispered.

Trace brushed his knuckles up her cheek. "Have I ever lied to you?"

"No, but—"

"Hey." He brushed her hair back, framing her too-solemn face in his hands. "For your information, lady, I've always been wild about self-made women. Especially successful, sexy, self-made women." He grinned—that quick, boyishly appealing grin she'd been afraid she'd never see again. "And if you want to know the truth, I can't wait for you to become a world-famous restaurateur so you can support me in the style to which I have every intention of becoming accustomed."

Despite the fist that still had a death grip on her heart, Hannah managed a shaky laugh. "You're good for me," she said, unable to keep the love from shining in her eyes.

"I believe that's what I've been trying to point out."

"And I do love you."

"Ditto."

She arched a dark brow. "Ditto?"

Trace looked at her in mock surprise. "Oh, did you want me to say the words? Again?"

"I don't think I could ever get tired of hearing them," Hannah admitted.

Trace shrugged. "Well, since you put it that way..." He gathered her in his arms and pressed his lips against her temple. "I love you." He kissed her eyelids. "Love you." Her cheeks. "Love you." Her chin. "Love you."

The heartfelt words, along with the snowflake-gentle caress of his lips, caused a renewed warmth to flow through her. Hannah linked her arms around his neck. "I love you," she repeated, finding the words easier each time she said them. "And I want you."

His lips feathered at her ear. "And I want you, too, sweetheart. But there's just one little thing we have to get out of the way, first."

"I'll help," Hannah said, reaching for the drawer where Trace had moved in a supply of condoms.

He caught her wrist. "Not that. First I want to know if you're going to marry me."

"I . . . I thought I explained all that," she stammered.

"So you did." Heaving a deep, regretful sigh, Trace pushed himself up from the bed and began to dress.

She stared up at him in disbelief. "What are you doing?"

He pulled on a pair of white cotton briefs. "Going home." His jeans were next, followed by the forest-green wool shirt Hannah had insisted on buying for him in

Phoenix. She'd been drawn to the shirt the moment she saw it in the window shop in the hotel lobby; the color had reminded her of his eyes when they made love.

"But I thought you were going to spend the night."

"I was," he agreed. The mattress sagged under his weight as he sat down to put on his wool socks and boots. "But I've suddenly discovered that I'm a greedy man."

"Greedy?"

He stood up again, his eyes gentle but firm. "I love you. And I want more from you than a few stolen hours, Hannah."

"But that's what tonight is about. We agreed that you were going to stay the night. All night."

He shook his head. "Sorry. It's still not enough. I want all your nights, Hannah. Every single long, love-filled night, for the next fifty or sixty years." Despite the serious turn the conversation had taken, he surprised Hannah by smiling broadly. "Did you know that the sixtieth anniversary is diamonds? I figure if I start saving now, by the time I'm ninety-five, I should be able to afford a pair of earrings to match Grandmother Murphy's ring."

Hannah stared at him, searching for the joke. She couldn't find it. "You're crazy, Trace Murphy."

"That's what they say," he agreed amiably. He bent down and gave her a quick, hard kiss. Hannah pressed her fingers against her tingling lips as the brief flare ended all too soon. "I'll see you around, sweetheart. Call me when you've changed your mind."

Stunned, she watched helplessly as he strode across the room. She'd told him she loved him, hadn't she? Trace had always seemed so easygoing, why couldn't he just settle for that? For now. "Trace?"

Trace stopped in the doorway and closed his eyes, garnering strength before he turned around. He knew what he'd see: Hannah, sitting amid the love-rumpled sheets, looking delightful, delicious, delectable, and most dangerous of all, vulnerable. It was that soft trace of vulnerability, which she tried so hard to conceal, that he found almost impossible to guard against.

"Change your mind already?" he inquired pleasantly. Her eyes were wide, lustrous, eloquent in their need. It took every bit of self-restraint Trace possessed not to give in to their silent plea.

She wanted to. But some last mental barrier lingered, and she couldn't quite overcome it. She needed time. Time to sort things out. Time to envision herself as a wife again. "What about the ring?"

Stifling a sigh, Trace told himself that he shouldn't have expected Hannah to give in right away. "Keep it," he suggested with a careless wave of his hand. "Maybe after you get used to having it around, you won't feel so threatened by it."

With that he was gone. Hannah didn't make a move to stop him, convinced it had to be some sort of bizarre joke. She heard the Jeep start up and drive away, but still she waited.

The only sounds in the room were the steady tick-tick-tick of her alarm clock and the painful beating of her heart. Somewhere in the distant hills, a lonesome coyote called out to the full moon. The sad song stimulated a similar response among the neighborhood dogs; next door the Walkers' German shepherd joined in mournfully to the chorus. Still Hannah waited.

THE MIDNIGHT-BLUE OF THE SKY turned to pearly gray, then dusty rose as the sun crept over the horizon. Hannah was sitting in the middle of the bed, wrapped in sheets that still carried the evocative scent of their earlier lovemaking. A new day dawned. Hannah forced herself to accept the fact that Trace wasn't coming back.

Hannah's method of working out difficult decisions was quite basic. She cooked. Every bowl, pot and pan in her kitchen was utilized as she created mountains of food she had no intention of eating: wafer-thin crepes wrapped around plump strawberries and drenched in powdered sugar; buttermilk-almond biscuits; plump Belgian waffles. She was beating some eggs into a golden froth for French toast when someone knocked at the kitchen door. Her fingers tightened on the wire whisk.

Trace. She'd known he couldn't stay away.

She flung open the door, her face falling as she saw Mrs. MacGregor standing on her back porch. Sometime between the strawberry crepes and the Belgian waffles, she'd decided to marry Trace. As soon as the State of Arizona allowed.

"Oh. Good morning."

"Morning," the woman said agreeably, trying to look around Hannah. "Something sure smells good."

Remembering her manners, Hannah opened the door wider. "I was just making breakfast and I'm afraid I got carried away. Perhaps you'd like to share it with me."

"Well, gee, that'd be right nice, but the real reason I came over here is to—" Mildred MacGregor's voice drifted off as she stared at the vast array of dishes covering the countertops. "Gracious. I can't remember when I've seen so much food in one place."

"You're welcome to help yourself. I was, uh, just trying out recipes for the Red Rock."

Mrs. MacGregor's eyes brightened as they settled on a cinnamon and pecan coffee cake Hannah had just taken from the oven. Hannah could practically see the elderly woman's mouth begin to water. "Well, if the stuff you serve at the café is anything like this, you're gonna be a real hit."

"Thank you," Hannah said, taking down a plate from the cupboard and placing it on the table. "What can I do for you?"

Mrs. MacGregor pinched a corner off a golden-brown biscuit, rolling her eyes as the airy dough practically dissolved in her mouth. "Do?"

"You said you'd come over here for a reason," Hannah reminded her as she placed a fork, knife and napkin beside the plate. Although her heart was still heavy from her disagreement with Trace, she managed a slight smile. "Although if you're here to borrow some eggs or butter, I'm afraid I'm flat out."

"Glory be," Mrs. MacGregor exclaimed around a mouthful of corn fritters, "I nearly forgot. It's Trace."

Hannah's blood went cold. "Trace? Is he all right?"

"Well, sure. Leastwise for now, but the way that Jake Brennan's been actin' up, you just never know what's going to happen."

"Jake?"

"He escaped from jail last night, after Cal took him back from the party. Seems they were playing poker when he just reached over and pulled Cal's revolver from his holster with nary a please nor a thank you, then locked him up in the cell and took off. Nobody knew a thing about it till Trace stopped by this morning with some glazed doughnuts from the doughnut shop over in Cottonwood." She eyed the abundance of dishes appraisingly. "I'll bet if Jake had been promised some of this stuff, he would've hung around at least till after breakfast."

Hannah's heart was beating a hundred miles a minute, and thunder roared in her ears. "Did Trace go after him?"

"Well, of course. After all, that's a sheriff's job, ain't it? Chasing down escaped convicts."

Hannah pressed her fingertips against her temple. Her head was spinning, she had to think. "I have to go to him."

"I kinda figured you'd want to do that," Mildred MacGregor said pleasantly. "He's out at Jake's place, on the old river road just outside of town. Seems Jake's determined to have some sort of showdown with those government officials when they come to auction his place off."

"Oh, no," Hannah breathed. "I take it he's got more than just Cal's service revolver."

Mrs. MacGregor bobbed her gray head. "The way I hear it, he's got a shotgun," she confirmed. "Been taking potshots out the window all morning." If that wasn't bad enough, the elderly woman's next words sent ice water through Hannah's veins. "Leastwise he was until Trace went into the house. Things have quieted down considerably since then."

"Trace is in the house with him? Alone?"

"Sure is. After all, it's—"

"Part of the job," Hannah finished, yanking her parka from its hook. "I know." Running back into the bedroom, she plucked the velvet box from the tangle of sheets. She was halfway out the door when she came skidding to a halt. "I can't believe it, I almost forgot about Scott. Mrs. MacGregor, would you mind. . . ."

"That's what I came over here for," the woman confirmed with another nod of her head. "To stay with the boy while you go stand by your man."

Her man. Hannah was amazed at just how wonderful that sounded. Trace was her man. Just as she was his woman.

"Thank you," she said. "And please, help yourself to anything you want." As Hannah ran out to her car, Mrs. MacGregor's gaze swept happily, hungrily over the room.

THE RANCH HOUSE, situated in a grove of trees and surrounded by serene white fields of snow, looked like something from *Little House on the Prairie*. Only the police cars representing the law-enforcement agencies of three adjoining counties, along with the Department of Public Safety, a number of government vehicles and brightly colored news vans from the Prescott and Flagstaff television stations, revealed that the setting was not as peaceful as it looked.

"Dan," Hannah cried out, spotting the older man in the crowd, "what's happening?"

Dan Murphy, with a grave-faced Mitzi by his side, made his way through the throng of people to Hannah's side. "He'll be all right, Hannah," he assured her. "Jake would never hurt Trace."

"You can't know that," she insisted. "Not for sure. What was Trace thinking of, going in there like that?"

"He was trying to keep an old friend from getting in worse trouble than he already had," Dan said simply. "Along with wanting to keep some innocent person from getting hurt."

"What about him?" she said, frustrated by the way first Mrs. MacGregor and now Dan were taking Trace's behavior so matter-of-factly. "Isn't he an innocent party?"

Dan looked momentarily surprised. "He's the sheriff," he said, as if that explained everything.

Mitzi put her arm around Hannah's shoulders. "Trace is one of the smoothest talkers I've ever met. He'll have Jake putting down that gun before all those cops' morning coffee gets cold back at the station."

"Damn him," Hannah swore, furious that he would dare to risk his life before she had a chance to accept his proposal. Before he could see her wearing his grandmother's ring. "If he gets out of there alive, I'm going to kill him."

"Spoken like a woman in love," Dan observed with the same easy humor Hannah had come to love in Trace. "Mitzi never makes any sense these days, either."

"You're both damn lucky we put up with you," Mitzi shot back. "The whole town knows that the Murphy men have always been crazy, beginning with old Jedidiah."

"Guess that's what makes us so irresistible," Dan drawled. He smiled encouragingly down at Hannah. "He'll be all right, honey." This time it was Trace's unfailing optimism and confidence she heard in his father's voice. As Hannah watched the SWAT team arrive in their armored van, she could only hope he was right.

THREE HOURS. Jake had managed to hold that shotgun on him longer than Trace ever would have thought possible. He wasn't at all afraid that Jake would shoot him; he was, after all, the man who'd been married—albeit for too short a time—to Jake's daughter. No, he'd never pull that trigger, but knowing that didn't make Trace any less tired of staring down that double barrel.

"Almost nine o'clock," he said conversationally, looking up at the clock on the mantel. "The federal offices will be open soon."

He'd told Jake about Karen Fairfield, told him about the records the woman had pored over, told him about the entries she'd found which had mistakenly credited Jake's payments to another account and the lawyer who'd worked all night preparing an injunction to halt the auction. Having suffered too long in the tangled bureaucratic web, Jake wasn't going to believe any of it until he talked to Karen Fairfield and the judge himself.

Jake glanced out the window.

"I wouldn't do that, if I were you," Trace said quietly.

"Do what?"

"Start shooting out the window again. They've brought in a SWAT team from the city. You could end up getting us both killed."

Jake reached into his pocket with his free hand and pulled out a pack of cigarettes. Shaking one loose, he held the pack out toward Trace, who declined. "So what?"

Trace leaned back in the hard chair and forced himself to relax. Ten more minutes. His legs were starting to go to sleep, and his tailbone felt as if it was resting on a rock.

"Well, maybe you don't have anything to live for," he said. "But once I get things buttoned up here, I intend to get married."

"To Hannah."

Trace wondered if he'd made a tactical error, mentioning his plans to remarry. "She's a nice woman, Jake," he said with careful casualness.

The older man drew on the cigarette and its red tip flared; a cloud of blue smoke filled the air between them when he exhaled. "Seems to be," he agreed. "Little skinny, though. She don't have a lot of meat on her."

"Ah, but what the lady has is choice," Trace pointed out with a grin.

Jake chuckled. "I always liked you, Trace. You treated my Ellie real nice. Even if you weren't good enough for her."

It was Trace's turn to chuckle. "As far as you were concerned, there wasn't a man in the state good enough for
Ellen Brennan."

"True enough," Jake confirmed. "She was a sweet girl,
wasn't she? And pretty."

"She was sweet," Trace said. "And beautiful. And I
loved her a great deal."

Jake studied the ash at the end of his cigarette. "Never
said you didn't. So now you love this widow woman."

"Hannah," Trace confirmed. "And yes, I love her. Does
that bother you?"

"Maybe a little," Jake decided. "But only because I wish
things could've turned out different. With you and Ellie."

"We can't always choose the way our life's going to turn
out, Jake," Trace said quietly. "Although in this instance,
I'd say you're holding both our futures in your hands." He
reached over, picked the telephone up from the table and
handed it to the older man. "Make your call."

TIME CRAWLED BY at a snail's pace as the crowd of spectators behind the orange police barricade increased. When
there was still no action to film from the house, the television cameras began grinding away, forced to settle for
reporters doing stand-ups in front of the gate. Dan had
refused any interviews. The frighteningly well-armed
SWAT team was eagerly poised for action, planning strat-
egies, checking weapons.

The storm had passed during the early hours of the
morning; the day had dawned clear and bright and sunny.
It was a day for laughing, for loving. Not for dying. A
handsome young deputy from neighboring Coconino
County offered her a cup of coffee from a Styrofoam cup;
Hannah politely refused, her gaze riveted on the ranch
house. Mitzi suggested she go and wait in Dan's truck,

where she could get out of the cold; Hannah wasn't about to move. Cal Potter, looking twenty years older than he had while singing off-key at the party last night, offered what Hannah guessed to be an apology for allowing Jake to escape. Although she couldn't hear the words, with the thunder roaring in her ears, Hannah put her hand on his arm and murmured reassuring words she wished she could believe.

But she never took her eyes from that front door.

Finally, after what seemed an eternity, the door opened. Hannah was unaware of holding her breath until she released it with a ragged, painful sob. Then, ignoring the warnings of the lawmen, shaking loose the deputy who tried to stop her, she leaped over the barricade, burst through the gate and was running across the soft white expanse of snow between them.

"You're all right!" she cried, flinging herself into Trace's arms. "You're safe."

Trace had dropped the shotgun into the snow in order to catch Hannah as she came hurtling toward him. As she smothered his smiling face with kisses, he decided it could stay there a while longer. "Of course," he said as he lowered her to the ground. "Don't tell me you had any doubts?"

"Doubts?" She laughed because she could no longer cry. "Damn you, you had me scared to death . . ." She turned on Jake, her eyes shooting angry sparks. "And you," she said, poking her finger into his chest, "how could you do something like this? To Trace? To me? Don't you know how he cares for you? How we all care about you?"

A crimson flush rose from Jake Brennan's collar. "I guess I kinda found that out," he said sheepishly. "Turns out the government made a mistake."

"Well, that's certainly no surprise," Hannah said. "And it's certainly no reason to hold your best friend hostage."

Jake rubbed his unshaven jaw as he gave Hannah a long, appraising look. "The woman speaks her mind," he said finally.

"That she does," Trace agreed.

"Probably gonna be a handful."

Trace nodded. "I'm counting on it."

Jake shrugged. "Everyone always said you Murphys were crazy."

"That's what they say, all right," Trace acknowledged cheerfully.

"Takes all kinds," Jake muttered with a shake of his head. "You two take your time. Guess I'd better go turn myself in."

Trace reached out and put a hand on the smaller man's shoulder. "I'll do what I can to get you a reduced sentence for this latest escapade," he said. "The way I figure it, you didn't really threaten anyone. For all anyone knows, you could've been shooting at coyotes."

"I was," Jake muttered. "The human kind."

"Let's just keep that to ourselves, all right?"

"So long as I know my land's gonna be here when I get out, I don't mind spending some time in jail. You gonna be doing the cooking?" he asked Hannah.

"Yes, although after what you put me through this morning, I'm not sure you're going to like it."

Jake's eyes narrowed suspiciously. "You wouldn't."

Hannah nodded. "Yep. We're talking bait."

"Mebee I can swing a deal to get sent to the State pen," he mumbled, shuffling away through the snow.

"Bait?" Trace asked, putting his arm around her waist.

"It's a long story."

"I've got plenty of time."

"That's right. If I remember correctly, you said something about fifty or sixty years," she said as they walked toward the throng of onlookers.

"At least." He lifted her left hand. The diamond sparkled in the bright winter sunshine. "I like this ring. It looks kind of familiar."

Hannah tilted her head back to look up at him. "I like it, too. Enough that I've decided to stick around for the matching earrings."

"Greedy," Trace teased as he nibbled lightly on her smiling lips.

Hannah threw her arms around his neck. "Wait until I get you alone," she promised, "and you'll find out exactly how greedy I can be."

A rousing cheer went up from the spectators as their lips met and clung. "Come on, Sheriff," she said, linking arms with him as they continued toward the Jeep, "I've got breakfast waiting back at the house."

"Sounds great," Trace said agreeably. "What are we having?"

Happy endings did exist after all, and not just in fairy tales. Hannah's answering laughter was free and breezy. "It's a surprise."

Harlequin Temptation

COMING NEXT MONTH

#237 HOW SWEET IT IS!
Roseanne Williams

Cookbook author Cait Rafferty adored chocolate in any way, shape or form. Then superhunk Adam Webster jogged onto the set of the TV talk show where they were both appearing. And Cait realized there were other things in life that are sweeter by far....

#238 GONE FISHIN' Elizabeth Glenn

Working at her family-owned fishing camp gave Bronwyn Jones a rewarding sense of peace—until Jefferson Clayton Smith IV started making waves in her pond. She knew she wanted him badly, but having him meant making drastic changes in her life....

#239 A SIMPLE "I DO" Joanna Gilpin

Gail Sheridan was happy to decorate Alec's home/clinic, and delighted to share his bed. She even loved his son as her own. But never would she marry a man whose proposal came in the form of a legal document....

#240 BE MINE, VALENTINE
Vicki Lewis Thompson

Roxie Lowell refused to believe there was anything predictable about her love life. Her falling for Hank Craddock simply couldn't have been engineered by that old eccentric Charlie Hartman, even though he claimed to be St. Valentine himself. Then again, Charlie was as mysterious as Hank was irresistible....

Harlequin Temptation dares to be different!

Once in a while, we Temptation editors spot a romance that's truly innovative. To make sure *you* don't miss any one of these outstanding selections, we'll mark them for you.

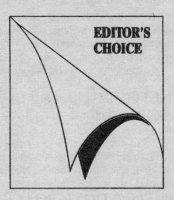

EDITOR'S CHOICE

When the "Editors' Choice" fold-back appears on a Temptation cover, you'll know we've found that extra-special page-turner!

THE

Temptation

EDITORS

Have You Ever Wondered If You Could Write A Harlequin Novel?

Here's great news—Harlequin is offering a series of cassette tapes to help you do just that. Written by Harlequin editors, these tapes give practical advice on how to make your characters—and your story— come alive. There's a tape for each contemporary romance series Harlequin publishes.

Mail order only

All sales final

TO: *Harlequin Reader Service*
Audiocassette Tape Offer
P.O. Box 1396
Buffalo, NY 14269-1396

I enclose a check/money order payable to HARLEQUIN READER SERVICE® for $9.70 ($8.95 plus 75¢ postage and handling) for EACH tape ordered for the total sum of $_____*
Please send:

☐ Romance and Presents ☐ Intrigue
☐ American Romance   ☐ Temptation
☐ Superromance   ☐ All five tapes ($38.80 total)

Signature_____

Name:_____
              (please print clearly)

Address:_____

State:_____ Zip:_____

*Iowa and New York residents add appropriate sales tax.

AUDIO-H

Harlequin Superromance

CALLOWAY CORNERS

Created by four outstanding Superromance authors, bonded by
lifelong friendship and a love of their home state: Sandra Canfield, Tracy Hughes, Katherine Burton and Penny Richards.

CALLOWAY CORNERS

Home of four sisters as different as the seasons, as elusive as the
elements; an undiscovered part of Louisiana where time stands
still and passion lasts forever.

CALLOWAY CORNERS

Birthplace of the unforgettable Calloway women: *Mariah*, free
as the wind, and untamed until she meets the preacher who
claims her, body and soul; *Jo*, the fiery, feisty defender of lost
causes who loses her heart to a rock and roll man; *Tess*, gentle
as a placid lake but tormented by her longing for the town's bad
boy and *Eden*, the earth mother who's been so busy giving love
she doesn't know how much she needs it until she's awakened
by a drifter's kiss...

CALLOWAY CORNERS

Coming from Superromance, in 1989:
Mariah, by Sandra Canfield, a January release
Jo, by Tracy Hughes, a February release
Tess, by Katherine Burton, a March release
Eden, by Penny Richards, an April release